SCAR ON THE MOON

SANDESH RAJ

ISBN 979-8-88909-959-8

Acknowledgement

I would like to acknowledge and give my warmest thanks to my editor, **Sudhir R**, for his immense support in completing my book.

Chapter - 1

On this frosty morning, the usually lush green landscape appears as if it is covered by a blanket of freshly made, white cotton candy. How everything can radically alter in a single night! The tops of the tall green trees, covered with a thick layer of fresh, fluffy white snow, appear as if old, wise men are standing quietly. A protective mother bird begins chirping in anxiety. She instinctively understands that in order to safeguard her young nestlings, mother will now need to labor even harder than before.

However, while the white snowflakes are a source of worry for some people, they are a gift from the sky for others. The atmosphere is filled with waves of laughter from happy children. These innocent blessings of God, pick up some snow in their cute little palms, shape them into snowballs, and fling them naughtily at each other. It is a giggle-fest all the way.

Chandrika is sound asleep in her soft, cozy bed, completely oblivious to the way the weather outside has altered in the course of the night. Chandrika's landline is constantly ringing, but she is not in the mood to pick it up. She simply sinks into her plush, comfortable blanket and drifts off to sleep once more. Unfortunately, her blissful state will soon come to an end.

The ringing does not stop. Only when the phone rings a third time and the annoying ringtone starts to irritate her, does Chandrika decide to answer the phone. She, however, is still very reluctant to leave the pleasant caress of her blanket and merely reaches out from beneath it. Her hand gropes for a while on the bedside table nearby. She finally locates the receiver, but when she tries to pull it closer the spiral cord tangles around her arm. She tussles with it till the cord gives way, and she tucks the receiver under the covers.

"Hello!" Chandrika barks.

"Hello? Are you still sleeping?" Chandrika's mother's scratchy voice is unexpectedly loud.

"Why have you disturbed me so early in the morning?" Chandrika's eyes are still closed while she scolds her mother. She wants the conversation to end as quickly as possible because she desperately wants to catch a few more precious winks.

"Listen, the city has been experiencing a snowstorm since last evening and everything has been shut down, including the highways and public transport. You do recall that you are traveling to Chandigarh today, don't you?"

Even if wildfires were breaking out, Chandrika couldn't care less.

She replies swiftly to prevent her mother from slipping in any more words, "Yes, Mom, I will arrive on time."

Before Chandrika hangs up, Phoola expresses her concern quickly, "My red *zari* (thread made from fine gold or silver wire) saree, on the top rack of the almirah—don't forget to bring it. Do you understand?" Phoola's tone calms down a bit as she places her request.

"Yes, Mom, I will for sure. Now let me sleep."

Phoola wants to talk some more but Chandrika ignores her and places the receiver back in its cradle. She wraps herself tightly inside the blanket with a big smile on her face. It takes only a few seconds for her to fall asleep again. However, as fate will have it, hardly five minutes pass when the phone begins to ring again. This time Chandrika replies more rudely.

"What is the matter now?!"

"Chandrika, behave yourself! I am SP (Superintendent of Police) Dogra speaking." These voice and words are enough to rouse Chandrika out of her sleepy trance.

"Sir?" Chandrika says as she springs out of bed without wasting a single second. She barely registers the cold outside the blanket as she shoots off her reply.

"*Jai Hind,* sir!"

"*Jai Hind!*" SP Dogra replies curtly and gets straight to the point. "Do you have a pen and paper near you?"

"Sir, just a second." Chandrika opens the drawer with trembling hands and grabs a pen and a notepad. She quickly turns to a blank page.

"Yes, sir, I am ready."

"You know Mrs. Varunika, who recently shifted to our city and stays near Shimla?"

Chandrika takes a second to recollect. "Are you talking about Varunika Dhawan, the famous model?"

"That is correct."

Chandrika thinks to herself, *how is it possible for anyone to forget the stunning woman with a flawless complexion, large eyes, curling hair, hourglass figure, brilliant smile, pearly white teeth, and so many other traits that make her a true diva?* Chandrika restrains her excitement though and pays attention.

"Currently, she lives in a resort outside the city. She called this morning to report that one of the three men staying at the resort is harassing her."

"Who are those three men? Did she register an official complaint?"

"Chandrika, this is a high-profile case and all investigations will be done offline. You must be aware, she is the daughter-in-law of the Home Secretary, Mr. A.K. Dhawan, and you will have to deal very carefully with this investigation. No leaks will be tolerated, especially to the local press."

"I would like to remind you that I am scheduled to meet a prospective groom today." Chandrika makes SP Dogra aware of her predicament in a calm voice.

However, SP Dogra cuts her off before she can finish and says, "I am aware of it, Chandrika. It was I who sanctioned your leave yesterday. This investigation will not take up much time; an hour or two at the most. In fact, you should welcome this opportunity to cast yourself into the limelight."

"Yes, sir."

"After that, you are free to go anywhere. Let me give you the address now."

"Sir, can you WhatsApp the address instead? Some of your words are inaudible due to static on my side of the line."

"The internet is down." SP Dogra sounds irritated.

Chandrika immediately looks at her mobile screen and observes that no network bars are seen. She quickly slides open the thick curtain in front of a window. The sight outside disappoints her. Snow is everywhere and the sky is covered with dark clouds. She suddenly realizes that the lamp connected to the inverter is on. She immediately presses the remote button to check the TV, but its screen is blank too. Those clues are enough for her to judge SP Dogra's mood. She plugs the telephone charger forcefully into the wall-socket and asks, "Sir, please give me the address."

He dictates, "Sky View Resort…"

"I want to tell you a few more things," he continues. "Write down my landline number too. We will communicate only on that number. Head Constable, Girdhari, will join you."

"Okay, sir."

"Any doubts?"

"No, sir," Chandrika replies in a firm voice gathering that the call is about to end.

"Good."

"*Jai Hind,* sir!"

The SP disconnects the call.

Her earlier plan to get a few more moments of precious sleep are now shattered. All her ears can hear is the ticking of a countdown clock.

⁂

Chandrika completes her morning routine except for her seven-kilometer run. She quickly puts on her khaki uniform and prepares to head out. Somehow, she does not appear completely happy to have joined the police force as she had hoped for a different career earlier in her life. A dream career where she could travel around the world, when every time she uploaded a picture from a new location to Facebook, countless people would 'like' it.

Chandrika boils water in an electric kettle, makes some strong black coffee, applies a thick layer of yellow butter to a slice of bread and takes a bite. That the proud lady inspector keeps her uniform in ship-shape is evident from the ever-so-shiny belt. With half of a sandwich on a plate, she stands in front of a big mirror, ties her hair into a neat bun and holds it in place with a black net. She then adjusts the police cap to sit just right on her head. She pulls on a thick brown jacket to protect her from the weather outside, and a pair of black leather gloves.

In one hand, she holds a big bowl of lukewarm milk and in the other, another slice of bread. She locks the main door and puts the bowl of milk down. As soon as she does that, a large brown cat charges up and immediately begins to sip the milk. She pats the cat on the neck and gives her some bread as well. Though she would like to spend more time with the cat, duty calls.

The verandah is home to a well-kept red motorcycle. Chandrika places her cap in the storage box and straps on a helmet. At first, the bike refuses to start and appears to not want to leave its comfort zone. A couple of attempts later, it lets out a roar accompanied by white dense fumes of exhaust. Chandrika takes off, zig-zagging through the narrow roads of Shimla. Piles of snow line both sides of the road.

❧❧❧

Chapter – 2

26 Years Ago…

Kuber Rajput used to work in the State Department of Agriculture. One day he got an opportunity to visit the State of Chhattisgarh, particularly a tribal area, with the express purpose of educating natives on how to increase agricultural output through the use of cutting-edge technology.

The department had arranged a guesthouse for him. While he was there, a woman from the Gonda tribe, Subhadra, regularly visited the guesthouse to take care of the household chores. She also prepared the meals, cooking food that was too spicy for Kuber and invariably upset his stomach. Kuber had no choice but to eat it. She brought her nine-month-old daughter along too because there was no one at home to take care of her. One of the several landmines set up by the Naxalites had claimed the life of her spouse. Subhadra had named her daughter Pakhi.

On some days, when Kuber returned early, he found that he had nothing much to keep him occupied. No groceries to buy, no books to read, no other chores to attend to. His only pastime was to shop at the weekly market, called *haat* in the local language. With no family to engage with and a village moving at a snail's pace, he found ample time to bond with the little angel, Pakhi. And as time progressed, the daily playtime soon morphed into a fatherly responsibility.

He played for hours with his newfound little one, changed her nappies, fed her, and rocked her to sleep when Subhadra was busy with her chores. Little did anyone know that fate had something totally different in store for Pakhi. One day, her mother went into the jungle to collect some dry wood and never returned. The villagers said that she may have been attacked and killed by a wild animal. As a result, Pakhi was sent to an orphanage and Kuber found himself alone again.

He missed her dearly. How can a doting father forget the captivating smile, the cute gurgles, the little hands that held on to his finger ever so tightly, and the innocent mannerisms that never failed to grab his attention. As memories of Pakhi tugged at his heartstrings, he decided to adopt her. Kuber called his wife, Phoola, and shared his idea. She was a wife who had not had the good fortune to enjoy motherhood yet and she readily agreed. Kuber completed all the formalities required to take Pakhi on a journey to her new home. The orphanage arranged for a lady, Kausalya, to accompany Kuber and help him with Pakhi on the journey, and also to ensure that Pakhi was heading to a safe and comfortable home.

☙ ☙ ☙

Phoola had been anxiously waiting since dawn and was beaming with excitement. She felt the passage of time go by extremely slowly. Her motherly instinct had taken over and she had decorated the house beautifully to welcome their newest family member. A few close relatives had gathered and were singing traditional songs to welcome the new arrival. Finally, Kuber reached his house and rang the doorbell. The moment that everyone had been eagerly waiting for had finally arrived. They were waiting for Phoola to open the door so they could shower the baby with rose petals.

Phoola greeted Kuber, her face wreathed in smiles. Her words could hardly make it out of her mouth, "Where is my adorable doll?"

Meanwhile, she spotted the dark-skinned woman holding a year-old baby that was squealing with joy. Kuber tried to introduce Kausalya but Phoola was too excited. Kuber had anticipated *an explosion more intense than Hiroshima; only this one would be of happiness and love.*

Kuber showed his hands to Pakhi, and said in a loud voice, "Meet our daughter."

Kuber had been trying to think of a modern name for Pakhi and as he peeped inside the house, he found it. There, written on the wall, were the words, '*Welcome Chandrika*'. (*Chandrika* literally means *moonlight*.)

"What?? She is Chandrika?" Phoola was shocked and smacked her forehead. She was expecting an angel, fair like the snow on mountains.

Phoola's younger sister, Deepa, caught a fleeting a glimpse of the little baby girl and was brimming with excitement to see her properly.

"Didi (elder sister), Didi, show me my niece!"

Deepa's excitement, however, diminished when she saw the girl's face.

Kuber looked at Kausalya, who looked very tired from the long journey throughout which she had cared for Pakhi. Kuber instructed Deepa to take her inside, which she unwillingly agreed to.

Phoola pulled Kuber aside, forgetting the long journey that he had just been through and asked him furiously, "Is this piece of charcoal the only one you could find in this whole wide world?"

"Why? What is the problem with her?"

"Go right away and drop it off back where you picked it up from!" This time Phoola sounded angrier.

"I cannot do that now. I have already completed the legal formalities." Kuber looked very frustrated.

"So what?"

"Try to understand and think about my government job too," Kuber replied calmly as he entered the room and greeted everyone. Kuber was very happy, but when he saw that no one else was, he could not enjoy the moment. A few traditional songs were sung hurriedly and the guests disappeared, one after the other. Phoola insisted that Deepa stay for a night, but she made an excuse and left.

It appeared for a while that communication between Kuber and Phoola had broken down. Kausalya sensed the problem and she chose not to intervene in their private matters. The next day, Kuber sported a long face as he accompanied Kausalya to the bus station. Since he didn't expect Phoola to care for the little darling, Chandrika, while he was away, he carried her along as well.

Kausalya clutched Pakhi tightly the whole time while the poor baby slept peacefully on her shoulder. The time had come for Kausalya to leave and part from Pakhi. Being woken up suddenly, to move from Kausalya to Kuber, was a shock for the sleeping kid. She started crying and Kausalya knew that the return journey of the new father would be difficult. Even though she was reluctant to leave the child, she waved one last time before boarding the bus.

❧ ❧ ❧

Phoola was adamant that she wanted nothing to do with Chandrika, not even touch her. That was reason enough for Kuber to hire a nanny to care for the little soul. The nanny stayed with them in their house. She was around 30 years old and light-complexioned. Kuber also helped the nanny with some of her tasks when he had the time, including feeding Chandrika, changing her diapers, and many others.

As time went by, and word spread about the adoption, relatives, neighbors and friends began gossiping, and speculating on all kinds of unnecessary issues. *What kind of daughter has this Rajput family adopted? What conflicts are on between the couple? Is Kuber having an affair with the young nanny? Will Kuber divorce his wife?*

Usually, in a community people are always eager to give unsolicited advice and suggestions as that gives them a sense of superiority. The same thing happened to Phoola. Her so-called well-wishers from far and near began alerting her to the danger coming her way. *To them, it was like enjoying a good old-fashioned bull fight, where two bulls bash each other up while the onlookers have a good time.*

They poisoned her mind to their heart's content. They said things like, *maybe Kuber will settle down with the nanny who looks prettier than Phoola.* However, sometimes things go the other way and the victim benefits. And that is exactly what happened in this case. Phoola felt her relationship was under threat and decided that she would rather take care of Chandrika and keep Kuber to herself.

The tide began to change for the better, and it became favorable for Kuber too. To his luck, one fine day, a TV channel ran a day-long telecast of movies featuring stories where *the wives were left to fend for themselves while their husbands found other women.* To his pleasant surprise, when he returned home, Kuber saw his beloved Chandrika in the arms of Phoola. Kuber asked about the nanny who had already been fired by a jealous Phoola after a big quarrel. Kuber took this in his stride. He accepted the changes as the will of God.

***

Chapter – 3

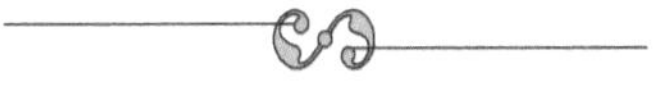

Pakhi's Story

I remember, when I was little, my father always spoke about inflation, the recession, global warming and many other interesting and sometimes sensitive issues. On the other hand, mom was only concerned about my skin tone. She was afraid *my complexion would get darker as I grew up, which would cause a lot of problems for me.*

One day, I asked, "Mom, I want to have some chocolate milk." I was only seven years old at the time. The reply I received was not only unbelievable to me then, but will be to you as well.

She said, "Pakhi, you should keep away from things like Bournvita, chocolates, Coca-Cola, tea, coffee, etc. After having those dark beverages, the color of your skin may turn darker, and then it will be very difficult for us to find a suitable groom for you."

Mom sounded harsh in the beginning but towards the end, her strong emotions turned to tears, like a person who is helpless and weak. I was too little to understand that her emotional reaction was brought about by my complexion.

" I want to chocolate milk… I want to… drink it!" I insisted stubbornly.

"What happened?" Papa reduced the volume on the TV and came to my rescue.

"Your beloved angel is insisting on drinking chocolate milk and other things that she must avoid. Look at her complexion now. She must understand that by drinking and eating things that are light in color, her complexion will lighten," Mom insisted, throwing me a woeful glance.

"That is all bullshit. There is no co-relation between what we eat or drink and its impact on our skin color. Science says our skin color depends on how much melanin is in our skin and I cannot see how eating and drinking can make much of a difference." My father supported me in a confident and stern tone.

"To hell with your science, which creates dirt in one's mind!" Mom said, bringing me a glassful of milk.

After smelling what was in it, I said, "Uhhhggg!" The smell caused me to shut my mouth tightly. Mom angrily placed the glass of milk on the table and covered it with a small steel lid.

"I am going to sleep. You give it to your daughter." Mom went straight to the bedroom without turning back.

Papa looked at me and tilted his head towards the glass. I knew at once what he meant. He inquired whether I wanted the milk or not. I scowled to show my dislike.

He then opened his almirah silently and took out a big jar. My eyes widened. Just as I was about to let out an excited scream, he quickly covered my mouth. Then he added a generous helping of Bournvita to the glass. I was greedy and asked for more. I justified my request by cupping his ear, and whispered,

"The whole of last week, I drank only plain milk. Hence, I deserve at least two spoons this time. Also, I don't want it just in the milk. I want some in a small bowl separately. I want to eat it too."

Papa scooped out two big spoons of Bournvita and served me. We both found immense joy: me from eating it and my father from watching the delight on my face. I twisted and turned my tongue to feel the texture of the powdered chocolate blended with sweet caramel. Opportunities like these were rare, since we could enjoy them only when Mom was not around. At all other times, I was restricted to having white food items only.

꙲꙲꙲

India has been facing the problem of casteism for a long time and strong laws have been introduced to curb the problem. In modern times, people talk about the progress made against casteism but not many address the still prevalent issue of racism and discrimination based on skin color. The only things that have changed are superficial like fairness creams being sold under less obvious names and the column for skin color being taken out of matrimonial ads. That, however, is just masking the issue. None of these things will bring our society to a turning point. Earlier, only women were soft targets. Now, savvy market players have understood that the obsession for fairness is universal and introduced fairness products for men as well. They received an overwhelming response, prompting the introduction of more products along those lines.

❦ ❦ ❦

Growing up in a society that discriminated based on skin color, I too was one among the many victims. Amongst my family and relatives, I was the only one who had a dark complexion. So, whenever I attended parties, weddings, or other social gatherings, people called me all sorts of names: 'black sheep among the white', 'black swan', 'crow', 'ugly duckling' and so on. I was made to feel inferior to anyone lighter-skinned.

At school functions, all the fair-skinned girls got opportunities to welcome guests and dignitaries. Moreover, they were photographed and featured in the local newspapers, and given opportunities to participate in the school events. Their parents collected these photos and showed them off proudly to relatives, friends and neighbors. It was the height of discrimination when the school published an advertisement for the new school session and only girls and boys with fair complexions got their pictures on the hoardings, with broad smiles on their faces, and books and bags in their hands. We carried the same books and bags as them but got no attention.

Mom strongly believed, that by using fairness products, anyone could turn their complexion from dark to fair and change their lives for the better. Every six months, or so, she changed my fairness cream, saying that the previous one was not doing a good job and she was hopeful that the next one would. She tried some home remedies too. Sometimes she mixed *besan* (chickpea flour) with *malai* (cream) and rubbed it over my skin. At other times it was turmeric, honey, rosewater and other kitchen ingredients made into a paste.

Sometimes, my mother compelled me to have sips of water from my cousins' glasses because she thought, *it would make my color become light like theirs.* I always refused to do so.

I usually did not like to apply any of those creams and pastes but one advertisement for a fairness cream touched my small heart. The commercial showed an old father with a ripped shirt asking for another cup of tea while reading the morning paper. His wife refuses. They cannot afford it as the father is in a low-paying job. Their dark-skinned daughter overhears this conversation and, at the same time, an advertisement for the job of an airhostess plays on the TV. She sees the airhostess, beautiful and fair-skinned, and realizes that because she herself is dark-skinned, she will never be able to clear the interview. To overcome her predicament, she begins applying a specific fairness cream and miraculously her complexion turns from dark to light.

Then the ad goes on to show how she impresses her interviewers and lands the airhostess' job. She then takes her father to an upscale restaurant where he demands his extra cup of tea, joyously.

Similarly, I too dreamed that whenever my father asked for one more cup of tea, post retirement, my mother would serve it to him happily. By then, I would have a high-paying job and we could afford a lot more. That thought sparked in me the ambition to land the job of an airhostess and encouraged me to use the fairness cream, even though I didn't like it.

❦ ❦ ❦

Mom also imposed a lot of restrictions on my activities, like preventing me from going outside in the hot sun, especially in summer. She warned me to stay at home lest I got tanned.

I had a neighbor, Nirmala aunty, her thinking was totally selfish and ridiculous. She used to request that I accompany her to the market in place of her daughter, Deepti, for fear that Deepti's fair complexion would get darkened if she walked in the sunlight. As for me, I was already dark skinned, how much more could the sun tan me?

This issue became a bone of contention between the two mothers. I was an innocent child and did not understand Nirmala aunty's intentions. Usually, my father was at hand to protect me from that sort of thing. As a result, I felt distanced from my mother. Her behavior irritated and frustrated me and I felt helpless as I could not control my skin tone and the fate that came with it.

ॐ ॐ ॐ

I'll never forget the time I was playing with my mother and fell. On that fateful day, I tripped over a plate, and its sharp edges cut the left side of my chin. I bled profusely. My father was out of station and mom took me to the doctor. He dressed and redressed my wound for the next 3-4 weeks. I remember, clearly, my mother weeping the whole night after the incident. The wound healed after a few weeks but it left a two-inch scar on the lower chin. According to Mom, that was even worse for my looks. However, when my father looked at my face, he smiled affectionately and said, *Scar on the Moon.*

ॐ ॐ ॐ

As I grew up, I understood that I was an adopted child and that's why I looked different from the others in my family. I also became aware of the harsh fact that there was no one left from my birth family, and I would never be able to go back to Chhattisgarh. It was a blessing from God that my adoptive parents were so kind and caring.

As time went by and I grew more mature, my mother's behavior did not bother me that much. Though her obsession with my skin color increased, I kept my cool. It was the attitude of others that irked me more. I was always put down and insulted at social gatherings but I didn't say anything.

My nature turned into that of a hermit who is often mocked and who never retaliates. I never expressed my anger.

My father, worried about the psychological impact all this might have on me, decided to send me off to boarding school. This happened when I had completed Class 8 with mediocre results.

Chapter – 4

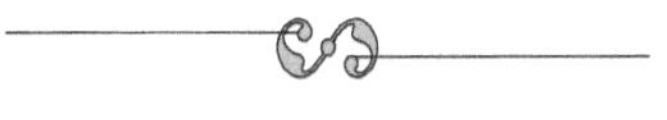

Things were pretty much the same at boarding school too. The only difference being that earlier I was teased by my relatives, now I was teased by students. Life, however, was good to me. I grew taller, my physique improved; good genes from my birth parents, maybe. But I didn't receive any praise for those qualities from my fellow students. My black skin was the only subject of their remarks along with my scar and extraordinary height. *Rakshasi, Shurpanaka, Lankini*, and other names were bestowed upon me. That did not faze me and I stopped myself from retaliating. I did complain to my teachers sometimes which made the students stop temporarily, but they just as easily resumed.

This state of affairs continued until I graduated from college. What people didn't realize was that I too was human. I had feelings just like everyone else and those comments made me sad and angry.

Once, when I was in Class 9 and it was wintertime, I went to a makeshift stadium in the school. There were a few rows of long step-benches, angled one on top of the other in the lush, green school playground, to resemble a small stadium. The rows of steps were curved and painted.

Students could sit on these rows to watch sports and other related activities. Usually, during my break time, I preferred to sit alone on those steps in the soft sunlight, watching other students play. I did not mingle much with my classmates on the ground though. I played sports too, mostly non-team sports. My first love was archery. I practiced with so much dedication that my fingers had blisters on them. I found that it was a perfect outlet for my anger, to channel it in a positive direction.

❦ ❦ ❦

It was a chilled-out Saturday, and I was enjoying my snacks on the stadium step-benches, when I noticed a Class 12 student whom I knew by face, passing by. I was curious and followed him. After walking a few meters, I came to an area with small trees and bushes. We usually did not venture into that area because, like every shadowy and mysterious place, it had its own ghost stories associated with it.

It was rumored that a spirit had made a place for itself on an old Banyan tree in the area and I suddenly realized that I was close to it. I swallowed the lump in my throat and continued to follow him at a distance. A few seconds later, he disappeared down the path, and I suddenly felt lost and afraid. I wanted to scream but my voice was stuck inside. Then, to my relief, after a couple of fear-filled seconds the boy re-appeared trailing five different-colored puppies. He took out some food and began feeding them. The sight of those little blessings of nature made me beam with joy and I could not hold back. I bent down and picked up one or two of them and they whimpered. They enjoyed themselves when I rubbed their backs and bellies. One of them cutely bumped his little black nose against mine and that feeling was like nothing else. I played with them till break time was up and then we both left for our respective classes.

Gradually, this became a routine, to follow my senior and have fun with the little balls of fur. This carried on for more than a month. My senior and I did not exchange a single word with each other and neither did I discuss the incident with my other schoolmates. It was my little secret.

The next Sunday was Valentine's Day. Adolescence is the age when the mind is very curious to explore new things. The school management used to allow students of each class to go into town on one Sunday of the month. This time it was the turn of Class 9. The excited girls had begun preparing a day earlier. They manicured and painted their nails, covered their faces with face masks and curled their hair to look more attractive. I too had a plan in mind. I was eager to talk to my silent senior and swap email addresses. I took out my favorite dress, placed it on the bed, and left the room on work.

To my annoyance, when I returned that I found that my roommate, Kavita, had already picked it up and worn it. I was seething in anger but Kavita just carried on completing her final touch up.

"Oh, Chandrika, I'm wearing your dress to town today," Kavita said blithely, when she noticed me. "You don't mind, no?"

"That dress was kept out as I was planning to wear it," I controlled my emotions and replied.

"Yeah? But what will you do even after wearing it? You rarely go outside, no one visits you and you have no one to show off your dress to. On the other hand, your dress will get some good compliments when boys see that I am wearing it. It is not important what kind of dress it is; it depends on who is wearing it and carrying it off. Once I go outside, just watch how the desperate bumblebees buzz around the pretty flower."

I was furious and wanted to slap that silly girl, but Neelam walked in and said, "Kavita you look so pretty. I'm sure your picture will be in tomorrow's newspaper with the headline: *A bunch of people died from heart attacks on seeing your unbeatable beauty.*"

"Oh, really!?" Kavita's ego knew no bounds and she turned around again to admire herself in the mirror.

"But I don't think anyone is jealous of you know who…" Kavita tilted her head towards me. Neelam understood clearly who she was talking about.

"Your dress looks so pretty! When did you buy it?"

"My mother gifted it to me," Kavita lied blatantly.

"Shall we leave, Kavita?" Neelam was excited to go out.

"Oh, yes!" Kavita gave me a dismissive look and that was enough for Neelam to sense that something was wrong between us. She left after scowling at me.

I looked at the mirror and angrily tried to rub my face but it remained the same. I sat down, wept, and decided it was better to stay in the room itself.

❦ ❦ ❦

Soon it was Monday afternoon, and the weather became quite pleasant. Spring had begun and new leaves were getting ready to sprout. The trees looked pretty with their covering of small green leaves. Break time was almost about to end but my senior was nowhere to be seen. I went back to class after feeding the puppies.

❦ ❦ ❦

A week passed by but my senior did not turn up. I decided to go to where his class was, but who would I ask for? I did not even know his name. I mustered up the courage and reached the place where Class 12 sessions were conducted, only to find that all the classrooms were vacant. I approached a peon and enquired why this was so.

The peon replied, "Don't you know that all students have study leave? No more classes. They have gone home and will be back only after a month to write the exams."

I felt disappointed at this, "I was looking for a particular student."

"What is his name?"

"I don't know. Well, I will meet him here when he returns."

I began to leave when the peon said, "It's difficult if you don't even know his name. Some students might never come back here."

"Why not?"

"During the board exams, examination centers are most often swapped between schools. So, he might end up going to a different place to write his exams. Also, his hostel is outside the school premises and you will not be permitted in."

Meanwhile, the Principal called for the peon, and he replied, "*Jee Sahib.*"

I wanted to cry but the tears just did not flow. I ran as fast as I could to where the puppies were sheltered. Once the puppies smelt me, they came running out, whimpering. I leaned against the bark of a tree, buried my head in my hands, and wept woefully.

Chapter - 5

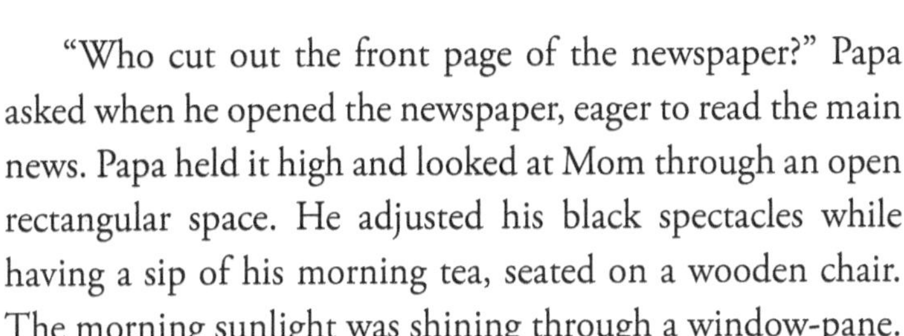

"Who cut out the front page of the newspaper?" Papa asked when he opened the newspaper, eager to read the main news. Papa held it high and looked at Mom through an open rectangular space. He adjusted his black spectacles while having a sip of his morning tea, seated on a wooden chair. The morning sunlight was shining through a window-pane. I was warming myself in the gentle rays of the sun while fumes of vapor were wafting from my glass of hot milk. I had returned home for my winter vacation.

"I don't know!" Mom ignored Papa and showed her irritation. She was busy peeling potatoes and had no time for useless things.

Finally, Papa turned to me and I admitted it. "I did it. Olivia Culpo won the Miss Universe title."

"I want to see that too." Papa was behaving like an eager child. Mom stopped for a moment and glared at Papa.

I interrupted to change the mood, "Papa your Miss Universe is in front of you."

"Of course…yes…yes! Your mom is my beloved," Papa stammered, and mom blushed for a moment before resuming her work.

Papa whispered when she went into the kitchen, "Where is that paper cutting?"

I drank my milk, placed the empty glass on the table and replied, "I have pasted it on my bedroom wall. She is very beautiful, isn't she?" I was very excited.

Papa glanced at his watch and realized he was running late, "It is already a quarter past nine. I will check it in the evening once I return."

I gave him a thumbs up.

❄❄❄

Present Day | 10:00 AM | Day 1

Chandrika stops her bike near the Sky View Resort, and Girdhari, the head constable, is already there. Girdhari is around 40 years of age, with a bald patch in the front of his head and thick hair everywhere else. He is light-skinned, of average height, and has a Chevron moustache style. To freshen his breath, he pops a green cardamom pod into his mouth. As soon as Girdhari spots Chandrika, he goes up and salutes her with a distinct lack of energy.

"*Jai Hind,* madam."

"*Jai Hind…*" Chandrika replies warmly. "Girdhari, did you not sleep well last night?" Chandrika asks, while eyeing the resort blanketed in fluffy snow.

"Nothing like that, madam. Today is my son's birthday and I stayed up all night decorating his room to give him a surprise in the morning and see the happiness on his face. I was asked to report for this investigation before I could catch even a few winks. Once this is over, I am going request that my landline be disconnected!"

Girdhari crushes the black seeds in his mouth in frustration. "Shall we go inside?"

The resort is situated on a small bypass road which the government is yet to widen. Only a few vehicles pass by on that route and those are the only people who know about it. It spread over 8-10 acres of land, surrounded by a four-foot wall. All of the guest rooms are located in the center.

Chandrika is confused about where to enter from as there is no gate in sight. A small watchman's cabin is on the right-hand side is to their right and appears vacant. There are some steps and they are in such bad shape that no one can climb them.

Girdhari indicates with a nod that Chandrika should follow him.

❧ ❧ ❧

The *phak-phak* of the Enfield Bullet is loud, shattering the otherwise peaceful atmosphere. Ishwar, who works there as a cook, is around 45 years old and is short and stout. He runs out anxiously to the motorbike and wears his monkey cap to protect himself from outside weather. He places both hands together on his chest and turns alternatively towards Girdhari and Chandrika. Meanwhile, Chandrika removes the key from the ignition of her red bike and stands quietly.

"*Jee Sahib.*"

"I am here for the enquiry. You must be aware of it."

"Yes…yes…Shabnam told me to expect you."

"Who is Shabnam?"

"Madam's maid."

Girdhari parks his black bike in the shade. It is freshly polished with wax and has a glossy look. A small spot near the petrol tank catches his attention before he gets off the bike. He takes out a white hanky and rubs the spot several times. He then gets off and walks towards Ishwar, swinging a long wooden baton to show off his authority.

"Where are those three guys?" Chandrika asks politely.

"Which three guys, madam?" Ishwar goes blank for a moment and that is enough to provoke Girdhari. He asks him rudely, "*Teen londe jo madam ko pareshan karte hai.*" (Those three guys who have been harassing madam.)

Chandrika notices Ishwar trembling with fear. She signs to Girdhari, *be polite.*"

"Which madam?"

"Your madam."

Girdhari tries to be well-mannered but the variation in his tone is not that much.

"Varunika madam!" Ishwar says abruptly.

"She has complained that one of the three guys staying at this resort has been harassing her."

"Oh, you are talking about, Saransh, Ravi and Ashok sir," says Ishwar. "They all are good boys." Ishwar is puzzled as he still does not understand what the police are alleging about them.

"Good or not, that is for us to figure out," Girdhari replies curtly.

Chandrika indicates that he should be politer. Ishwar realizes that it is better to communicate with 'police madam' as she appears calmer and more composed.

"Let me show you the way." Ishwar leads them on. Chandrika looks up at the beautiful glassed-in cottage perched up the slope where a woman's head appears at the window watching the police enter the compound. Chandrika looks at her for a fraction of a moment and then moves on.

ॐॐॐ

Chandrika's Story

Five Years Ago…

I had completed my graduation and decided that I no longer wanted to be a burden on my family. My father insisted that I pursue further studies but I refused. I wanted to throw him a grand party as I remembered the advertisement about a girl who had taken her father to a posh restaurant. *It gives you an immense feeling of achievement and pride when you are young, have received and completed a good education, and believe that you will get a job soon.* I had decided on my choice of career: flying the friendly skies.

However, when I arrived at the walk-in interview for air-hostesses, my confidence was in shreds looking at the beautiful girls around me with their flawless, fair-complexions, perfect figures and impeccable makeup. I looked so different from them, a black stamen among white rose petals. Most of the girls grimaced when they saw me. As expected, I was rejected and came out with an even duller face.

Still, I did not want to give up and decided to check with the HR Coordinator. She was busy collecting resumes and directing candidates to different rooms for interviews.

"Excuse me, ma'am," I said softly but confidently.

"Yes?" She glanced at me for a moment, then she turned away; the number of applicants was high.

I asked her directly, "Why have I been rejected?"

"What did the interviewer tell you?"

"Ma'am, where is the interview room?" one of the participants interrupted.

"Go straight and it's the third room to the right."

"Thank you, ma'am"

I had a few moments and did not want to lose that opportunity, "He told me to try again next time, that's it."

The HR Coordinator shrugged as if to indicate she was helpless in the matter and could do nothing further.

"Ma'am, I came six months ago and got the same standard reply." I felt like I had nurtured a tree and, after waiting a long time, it still bore no fruit.

This time, the HR coordinator completely ignored me. She continued smiling at the others but for me, she had nothing that could heal my wound.

"Ma'am, this is my dream job and I must clear the interview to prove myself," I pleaded.

"Well, then there must be a problem with you, that's why you were rejected," the HR Coordinator said bluntly.

"Is it because I do not look like the others? Is that why I have been rejected?"

"If you already know, why ask me and waste my time?" The HR Coordinator wanted to get rid of me. She pretended that she had to get herself some coffee and went off. I, however, was determined and kept following her.

"Ma'am, there was nothing mentioned about skin color in the interview advert. Also, I watched a couple of interview videos where it said that air-hostesses with dark skin color cannot be stopped from achieving their ambitions."

"Look Miss, we are not running a charity over here. Also, the company is under pressure to not discriminate on the basis of skin color, that's why we have to recruit some of you. Look at yourself—not enough makeup and rough skin. On top of that, you have a scar on your chin. Compare yourself with others and things will be quite clear. Now, please don't follow me because I have to manage other things too." The HR Coordinator walked into a room and closed the door.

After that incident, I decided to look into other avenues like hotel management, teaching, radio jockey, coffee-shop worker, English translator and others. I was selected for a few of them but I did not last in any position for more than three months. Sometimes I was paid and sometimes not. I got fed up and decided to quit everything. I prepared for the IAS. After a year of preparation, I was unsuccessful there as well.

Meanwhile, my mother was trying hard to arrange my wedding but the demand for dowry was so high that my parents could not afford it. At last, the only option within my sights was to join the State Police Force. My father insisted that I try for the IPS (Indian Police Services) instead, but I now had a fair idea about my capabilities. I knew that clearing the prestigious exam was not within my purview. Finally, I was selected for the Himachal Pradesh State Police as SI (Sub Inspector). Despite all the ups and downs, my father was still so happy and proud. He informed everyone, his relatives, friends and neighbors. On other hand, my mother was not as happy about the job for the same old reason: *roaming around in the sunlight will make me darker and no one will want to marry me.*

I used to always think, *who cares about a stupid wedding? Weddings are all about money-making. They have become a business. I was surprised when the match-maker insisted I add 'wheatish complexion' to my biodata. When I protested that it was misleading, he replied, "It's is all about marketing." If I mentioned "dark skin", no one would come to see me, let alone marry me. One thing was clear, dark skin was directly proportionate to dowry. The darker the skin, the higher the dowry demanded.*

❦ ❦ ❦

Chapter – 6

"Papa, what brand did you bring today for the party?" I asked eagerly when I heard the creaking sound of the wooden almirah being opened. Papa took out a bottle and it was Jack Daniels whiskey. He put two whiskey glasses on the table. It was a good time to celebrate. Mom was out of station, attending a family function, and I had a whole week to go before heading off for a year of training.

I twisted the cap to open it and it made a sound—kad… kad…kad. The sweet aroma of bourbon wafted out with its rich woody undertone. While pouring the amber-colored liquid into the whiskey glasses, I took a whiff, closed my eyes, and said, "Umm…" I took the first sip and it was smooth, soft, with a tinge of sweetness. My father resembled a famous movie hero of the seventies, square-framed specs, a thick head of hair and an attractive personality. The only difference was that the movie hero had no moustache, but my father did.

***

My father sat at the corner of a big black sofa. I felt a little buzzed after downing a peg. I leaned my head on the inside of my arm which was on the other side of the sofa. Papa quickly stood up and supported my head like a pillow would. *If you drink and do not talk, it usually means it's a waste of money.* After about ten minutes, I was ready to have a second peg and finished half the glass at one go. My voice was slurring and my mouth was swallowing its words.

"Papa, do you remember that whatever the occasion, whether getting a new job or being rejected from an interview, you always brought home liquor to celebrate, each time more expensive than what you brought on the previous occasion."

My father took a handful of fried nuts coated with spicy chickpea flour, cracked them open, and replied, "Yes, my little daughter."

"Little? I have grown, Papa," I slurred.

"For me, you are and will always be little."

"No, Papa. Call me Lady Singham," I demanded.

"Okay…okay…my Lady Singham." Papa always did things that I liked.

"You are my good…Papa."

"Which was the first bottle?' I tried to remember but could not recall. I wanted to open the wooden almirah where all the bottles were placed. Papa signaled for me to sit back down and replied, "Old Monk Rum."

"Yes… yes… I expected you to buy Chivas Regal this time."

"That will be the next one." Even after two pegs, Papa was normal.

"No, Papa, this is it. Full stop. I do not want to give you any more trouble. You are my sweetest Papa." I turned to my father and hugged him tightly. *I can bear any loss in my life but not my father's.*

"What was that job you got offered?" he asked.

"Which one?"

"Weren't you hired to scare primary school students into keeping quiet if they were making too much noise?"

"Hahaha…. that one!" I laughed loudly.

"And what was your reply?"

"I said to the interviewer, 'It'll be better if we hang your photograph in every class. That way, the students will never create mischief and they will forget the meaning of playing pranks.' After that, she scolded me, and I showed her the middle finger."

My father laughed. "And what was that ad campaign?"

"Which one?"

"The 'Before and After' one."

"Oh yes, that was the local brand of fairness cream. First, they took a picture of my natural look, for the 'before' shot, and later on applied lot of Lily White foundation to lighten me up, for the 'after' shot. My skin itched so much that I left the photoshoot halfway. The photographer shouted and threatened to sue, but I didn't care!"

Papa laughed heartily. The very next second he looked into my eyes and said, "I know you are not happy with your current job and your dreams are different."

I turned serious, as if someone had touched a raw nerve. However, before I could reply, Papa explained his thoughts about my job, in a philosophical manner,

"I am not worried that you have quit so many jobs, instead I'm happy that you tried them in the first place. You don't know how much experience you have gained. Those things will help you in the future and will also firm up your final decision."

I nodded in acquiescence.

After his next peg, Papa, looking like Rajesh Khanna in Anand, continued, "Our destiny has already been decided by God. If you get this job, it means that something good is going to happen." Papa observed that I was not convinced by his theory.

"Can I ask you a question?"

"Yes, Papa," I replied softly.

"Have you ever been in love with anyone?"

"I love you, Papa" I hugged my father tightly after having a few more sips.

Papa laughed again, "Not me, stupid…someone special."

I stood up and said, "When I was in Class 9, I had a crush on one of my seniors." I was slurring even more by now.

"Did he know?"

"My dearest Papa," I jumped onto the couch and continued, "a crush is always one-sided."

"Okay… okay, continue." Papa was interested in knowing all about it. I straightened up once more and replied,

"Nothing happened; he left the school." My face went dull.

"Have you ever spoken to him after that?"

"No… ne…v… never," I slurred.

"Do you have a name…?"

"No, Papa… I don't even know his name." There was a trace of despair in my unstable voice. I settled down on the couch and said, "I don't think I want to get married either." *The constant rejections have been very tough to bear. Sometimes it feels like it's just a business transaction for them. They don't want a union of minds. All they are after is loads of dowry. And I know my father is not very well-to-do because he was honest at his job.*

"I'm not insisting that you get married. But I do believe that one fine day you will find your Prince Charming. He is certainly out there."

I shrugged, "Who knows?"

After my third peg, I stretched out on the couch and Papa put a thick blanket over me and kissed my forehead. He could see that I had the same pain that I had been living with for the past 26 years.

❧❧❧

Six Months Ago…

It was the last day of training and we had all gathered in a big convocation hall. After some time, a senior IPS Officer, Mrs. Dalal, came to address us. She was of average height with sharp eyes, sported a short haircut like that of a boy's, and was brimming with confidence. She checked the microphone first and followed up with a greeting for us all. She stood at the dais, fingers steepled into a triangle and a charming smile on her face.

"Good morning to all of you. Finally, the day has come when you will leave the safe zone off your training and move on to face the real challenges in the police force. When people usually join the Indian Police Service, they have quixotic views on what a police officer looks like and what work they do. These views are usually shaped by mainstream movies and other media. But as time rolls on and they become an integral and informed part of the system, their idealism wanes.

The first sign of that is when the new officer starts to think only about what his politician bosses want rather than what the law demands. In our country, VIP culture is very deep-rooted, especially as far as politicians go, and if you do not pay attention to them, it can hurt their ego deeply. I remember, back when I was posted in Jalaun District, there was a powerful MP (Member of Parliament), who had served in the ministry during his previous tenure. He instigated his followers through hate speeches and, as a result, a mob set ablaze a few coaches of a train.

I reached out to one of my subordinates and clearly instructed him to arrest the politician. As evidence, I told him to show the video that we recorded during the speech. I had no idea what awaited me. My subordinate not only refused to obey my order but also argued vehemently. He tried to convince me that the politician had already left town and that there was no need to pursue the issue. I had no other choice but to take matters into my own hands. The next morning, I reached the police station early and refused to budge till midnight.

Finally, the rest of the police staff understood that I would not leave the police station until some action was taken against that politician.

Only then did they wake up and somehow, they managed to find and bring the politician to the police station. I then sent him to judicial custody. When I enquired further, I found out that my subordinate had been in constant touch with the politician and had been lying to me all the while. Subsequently, the law found him guilty too and he was convicted. It took time but finally, justice prevailed.

Always keep in mind, if someone spends even one rupee on you, they expect to get ten times their investment's worth in return. For us, no charity, nothing, can stop an officer who is clear about his responsibilities, the permits and boundaries of the law, and is ready to pack his luggage when the time comes. Never give up!"

At the end of her speech, Officer Dalal flashed a broad smile and gave us a two thumbs-up. After that, the hall resounded with loud clapping. It was an inspiring speech for all of us and a directive for how we, as officers, must keep walking the paths of honesty and integrity.

Chapter - 7

I had already informed Papa that I was coming by train and was one of the few lucky officers to have been offered postings in their hometowns. I stepped down from the train and found that no one was present to receive me. Then, all of a sudden, I saw Papa, dressed in a blue waistcoat and a matching tie, followed by relatives and friends. He had asked someone to unroll a red carpet on the ground.

Everyone had colorful garlands in their hands and they were accompanied by a band playing welcome and congratulatory tunes. Suddenly, everything around me began to move in slow motion. It was like a dream. All eyes were now turned towards the new officer dressed in a crisp khaki uniform.

The people standing along the sides showered me with rose petals. I made eye-contact with Papa and communicated gleefully, *I knew, you were different from everyone else, and are, and always will be proud of me.* I had tears of joy in my eyes and at the same time, a smile on my face. It was a mix of overflowing emotions.

Papa had a broad smile. Once I reached him, I saluted him briskly as I would my superior officer. "Officer Chandrika reporting for duty, Papa." My father also got emotional and hugged me tightly, his chest swelling with pride. In that magical moment, everything stopped and I could only hear the band playing in the background.

❧❧❧

I could not sleep that night because my excitement levels were through the roof thinking about my first day at work, which was in Sector 4 of New Shimla. I wolfed down my breakfast, put on my freshly-ironed uniform and headed out. I found mom waiting with an *aarti* plate, as is the tradition in Indian households to mark the auspicious beginning of something new. She prayed for me. I looked at the smiles on the faces of my parents, put the keys in the ignition, and roared off on my bike to begin my new journey.

❧❧❧

"*Jai Hind,* sir." I saluted and greeted my senior warmly.

"*Jai Hind,* Sub Inspector Chandrika. Once you have completed your formalities, you must meet Head Constable, Dwivedi, who will accompany you to your first assignment at a nearby village."

"Yes, sir."

Do you have a bike?"

I nodded.

"Good." A senior officer was busy writing something in his register. Meanwhile, I stood in front of his desk firmly. After a few moments, the officer raised his eyes and saw me. He appeared as though he was deep in thought. Then he asked,

"Why are you here?"

"Sir, I need the case details."

"Dwivedi will explain those to you. You may go now." He got busy again.

"*Jai Hind,* sir." I left the room. After a brief introduction to my other colleagues, I completed my formalities and was ready to leave. I searched for Head Constable Dwivedi, who I found was having tea.

❧ ❧ ❧

"Take a left turn here, madam." The bike moved from the paved main road to an unpaved road, and I had to slow down. Head Constable Dwivedi, who was directing me was around 55 years old.

"Do you have the details of the case we are going to investigate, Dwivediji?"

"Madam, there is nothing to know. It's a land dispute between two families. Sukhvinder Singh and Balvinder Singh are neighbors as well as relatives. Sukhvinder has lodged an FIR against Balvinder stating that last evening Balvinder attacked him with a *desi katta,* (locally-made pistol). He fired one shot at Sukhvinder when he was on his terrace. Luckily the shot missed and struck the wall instead. As usual, Balvinder denied these accusations."

My first reaction was that of fear and shock and I wanted to exclaim, *oh my God,* but I controlled myself and replied,

"Okay…"

"So, we must record their statements to further investigate who is in the right and who is wrong. Based on that, an FIR (First Information Report), will have to be filed."

"Hmm…Where do I turn next?"

"Madam, to the right."

ર્ષ ર્ષ ર્ષ

When I met Sukhvinder and his family, they were all very frightened. I went to the terrace and looked around. I could clearly see the spot where the bullet had lodged in the wall indicating that the shot came from close range, perhaps even the top of a nearby house. However, when the Head Constable started to write the report, I observed that his version was quite different from what we had heard earlier. He wrote, *Sukhvinder Singh fired a bullet at his own wall and has falsely accused Balvinder Singh due to the existing property dispute between them, pending in court.* When Sukhvinder read the report, his face turned pale, and he refused to sign it.

"What is the matter? Why are you not signing it?"

"Madam, you please read this."

I had a glance, took Dwivediji to the side and whispered, "What have you written?"

"Madam, you are new here. Balvinder Singh has very good political connections. We have no other choice but to write the report in his favor."

"Listen Dwivediji, I am here to fulfill my duties and uphold the rule of the law. You cannot write such a false report. All the evidence is against Balvinder." I ripped up the fake report and ordered Dwivediji to write a new one with the whole truth.

"Madam, at least ask Negi sir before doing this."

"There is no need to ask anyone. What we are going to write is based completely on the evidence."

Dwivediji was not happy and kept reiterating, "*Madam, ek baar sir se poonch lete hai*" (At least consult sir once before writing this report). I paid no heed to his advice and instructed him to carry out my orders. After completing of the report, Dwivediji went aside and tried to contact Inspector Negi, but his phone was out of range.

Then, I gave the report to Sukhvinder and asked him to read it once more. I assured him that it was the actual report and he would get justice. That gave him some confidence and he was happy to sign it. Sukhvinder's wife put her palms together to thank me. I held her shoulder for a moment, which gave her comfort and assurance. She had been sobbing until then, but felt better now.

⁊⁊⁊

"Dwivediji, did you try to call Negi sir?" I knew Dwivediji would have tried to contact Negi sir for sure.

"No, Madam…"

I gave him a stern look.

"Uh… yes, Madam," Dwivediji stammered.

By now, my bike had reached the main road, "What did he say?" I turned around a little but my focus was on the bike.

"Madam, his phone is out of range. I could not get through."

"Okay, no problem. First, I will reach the police station and then I will ask Negi sir what to do next."

"*Jee*, madam." Dwivediji's unhappiness and reluctance was very evident in his tone of voice.

⁊⁊⁊

It was 3:00 PM by the time I reached out to Negi sir, but he was out of the city on some personal emergency. There was no one else at the police station as they had all left for a roundup. I had very little time to take action. I logged the

FIR and asked Dwivediji to come with me, but he was still parroting the same old statement: *Madam at least consult Negi sir before taking any action.*

"Dwivediji, Negi sir is not reachable. We have no choice but to make a decision in his absence," I replied firmly.

"Madam, we can wait for him."

"No, as I said before, we don't have much time."

"Madam, then can you drop me off?"

"Why, what's the matter?"

"I am suddenly not feeling well," he said in a low voice.

"Just five minutes ago you were quite well."

I understood that he was faking illness to distance himself from the case. I wasn't going to let him off the hook that easily. He asked me to stop the bike by the roadside and pretended to vomit. I could see that he was just putting on an act. He continued to linger by the roadside in an attempt to waste time.

The City Magistrate's office was about to close in half an hour. I decided that it would be better leave Dwivediji there and head for the office to get an arrest warrant issued. However, Dwivediji, crook that he was, had already warned Balvinder of the way things were going and Balvinder was readying to leave town.

I tried his house two or three times, but there was no response. I immediately circulated his picture to every checkpost with a copy of the arrest warrant. After quite a search, he was finally apprehended around 10:00 PM, just as he was about to cross the border. He was taken into custody. I was pleased with my actions. When I connected the dots, I could see the similarities this situation had to what Dalal ma'am had spoken about during her speech. At the same time, there was a constant anxiety in my mind as to what would happen the next day.

࿇ ࿇ ࿇

I reached the office as usual and everything looked fine except for one thing. My colleagues were staring at me, but nobody said anything. It felt super uncomfortable. One of my superiors instructed me to go Mall Road, which usually meant a kind of routine patrol. I adjusted my cap, sat in the police van and spent some time on Mall Road. I returned after two hours had passed.

࿇ ࿇ ࿇

I quietly entered the police station and signed the register. I then glanced at Negi sir's room. The door was closed, but I could tell that he was inside. I tried to pull my chair closer to my desk and the scratch of its legs dragging on the floor was enough to grab everyone's attention. I peeked at Negi sir's room while pretending to be occupied. After ten minutes, the Head Constable came to my chair and said, "Negi sir is looking for you."

"Right now?" I felt restless and wanted to release my tension.

"Yes."

I quickly stood up and walked to Negi sir's room. What I saw inside astounded me. Both, Balvinder and Sukhvinder were sitting in the room. I stood behind them, so they did not notice me. Negi sir was busy writing something in a file. The constable was writing the last line and that grabbed my attention. *The allegations I have leveled against Balvinder are all false. It was I who fired those shots with my air-rifle.*

Sukhvinder then signed the document. I was confused and could not understand what was going on. I wanted to gain their attention so I saluted in a rush and said loudly, "*Jai Hind*, sir!"

For a moment my eyes met Sukhvinder's but he immediately turned away with a face full of guilt.

"So, Miss Chandrika, as a result of your actions yesterday in not conducting the investigation in accordance with the law, a respectable citizen has had to face harassment for no fault of his. Look at the report… all the charges against Mr. Balvinder are baseless."

I read the report quickly, turned around, and stood next to the constable.

"Sir, I made a decision on the basis of the evidence available and the statements of the people we questioned."

"I understand that officer, but things are a different now. Take a look at the ballistics report."

Negi sir gave a paper to the constable who in turn, handed it over to me. I read it and was shocked at the change in the report. The previous report said that the bullet had been fired from an actual gun, now it said that the shot had been fired from an air-rifle.

"Sir, let me go there and investigate once more."

"This is ridiculous! Are you doubting our capabilities? Do you mean the report is incorrect?" Negi sir raised his voice and it was loud enough to be heard by everyone outside.

"That's not what I meant, sir."

"You must follow the orders or instructions given to you without deviating from them. That is why I sent Head Constable Dwivedi with you, and you ignored his advice."

The room went silent for a few moments. I felt insulted and ashamed in front of the others.

"Sir, can I go now?" Balvinder asked.

"Oh yes, sorry for the inconvenience," Negi sir said with a broad smile.

"*Accha ji*, (okay*)*" Balvinder folded his hands, but before moving out of the room, he looked at me for a moment and conveyed a message: *See my power. Better not mess with me again.*

I wanted to drag him to a jail cell right then, but my hands were tied. Sukhvinder shrank into his chair meanwhile. Negi sir was busy reading something on his mobile. After a couple of minutes, he looked furiously at Sukhvinder.

"Why are you still here? How much more time of mine do you want to waste? Get lost! And next time, beware of who you accuse. Otherwise, you might end up being our guest at this station, and it is famous for providing good hospitality."

"*Jee… jee,* sir!"

Negi sir instructed the constable to go bring a glass of water, as he needed a few minutes alone with me.

"Chandrika, from tomorrow onwards you will report to the Shimla Police Headquarters and your reporting officer will be SP Dogra."

"Yes, sir," I stood firm.

"Since you are a new recruit and this is your first mistake, I am not taking any action against you. I would not have been so lenient with the others. Your investigation was not up to the mark and that shows that you are careless about your duty."

"Yes, sir. What kind of work do I have to do there?"

"SP Dogra will guide you. Now you may leave."

"*Jai Hind*, sir!" I saluted Negi sir and quietly returned to my chair. The people who had eavesdropped on our conversation had already begun gossiping amongst themselves, and that made me very uncomfortable. I looked at my watch and it was around 1:00 PM. Time was passing very slowly. The day proved to be extremely lengthy and exhausting. I felt stuck to my chair and did not get a chance to get up.

That evening, I turned my bike towards Sukhvinder's house.

※ ※ ※

"Why did you change your statement at the police station?" I placed my empty teacup on the small center table and asked politely. Sukhvinder and his wife still were visibly traumatized.

Sukhvinder did not respond. He continued rubbing the tip of his thumb and index finger to release his stress and avoided any sort of eye contact with me. I asked again, this time in a friendlier tone, "Did anyone pressurize you to change your statement?"

This time Sukhvinder's eyes abruptly darted towards me and back. "Balvinder has powerful political connections. Through them, some goons began harassing us. They forced us to change our statement."

"Why did you not complain about that to the police?" I looked at Sukhvinder's wife as it appeared that he was not in a frame of mind to speak anymore.

"Who would we have approached? One of the senior inspectors came to our place and threatened us with dire consequences if we did not change our statement. If the law-and-order situation is like a lamb and the politicians and their lackeys behave like predators, we find it is better to surrender than get attacked," Sukhvinder's wife replied tearfully.

I patted her hand and decided to drop the matter. Sukhvinder came out to see me off. He folded his hands and said, "*Mafi Madamji*" (My apologies, ma'am). He kept his hands folded until I left the place.

꙰ ꙰ ꙰

It was the middle of the week when I reported to the Police Headquarters. I looked for SP Dogra's room, which was closed. I asked a peon to inform Dogra sir that I have come to join duty. The peon told me to wait outside. He came out after a few minutes and I was eager to know, *must I go inside or not?*

"Sir wants you to wait outside on the bench. He is busy at the moment."

I looked around me. A long, battered wooden bench stood outside the room in the twenty-foot wide corridor. The peon entered and exited the chamber multiple times and whenever he went inside, I thought I would be called in, but nothing happened. Then, a troop of senior police officers came to meet Dogra sir and after a few minutes, he left with them and did not come back that day.

During the course of the day, many people came over during office hours, senior police officers, politicians, VIPs, media people… Sometimes Dogra sir, himself, went out to receive the VIPs. His schedule was very busy. Now this turned into a routine every day. In the morning, I would ask the peon about meeting Dogra sir and he would give me the same standard answer.

At other times, Dogra sir did not come to the station at all, and I was left sitting there hoping in vain. The peon watched my activities and understood that I was undergoing some sort of punishment. Sometimes he was kind enough to gesture about having lunch, which I used to forget about. I opened my small steel box to get at some *chapatis* with *subzi*. It was embarrassing for me when other police officers, who were aware of my incident, passed through the passage. They stared at me while I tried to show all was well with forced smile.

Due to this situation, my behavior at home changed as well. I preferred to be cooped up in my room most of the time. Papa asked me many times what was wrong and I just told him that I was tired due to the new job. Papa, however, knew me very well and had understood that things weren't right at the workplace, but he was unable to advise me further as I refused to confide in him.

※ ※ ※

Three weeks passed, and that time was enough to break me down. I began to understand the ground realities of my job. Then, one day, Dogra sir came outside alone, and the peon gestured, *this is the time, you can introduce yourself.* I stood up quickly and followed Dogra sir. I turned up just in front of him and saluted courteously.

"*Jai Hind*, sir. SI Chandrika reporting, sir!"

My sudden appearance stunned him for a moment and he found himself unable to respond. The peon immediately came up and handled the situation, "Sir, this is the officer who has been coming to the headquarters every day and asking for you. She has been waiting outside on the bench for many days."

Dogra sir was in his mid-fifties, clean shaven, with grey hair thinning on his head and combed back. He was trying to figure out who I was, so I reminded him that Negi sir had sent me and must have informed him about it earlier.

"Oh yes! You joined recently, didn't you? You haven't even completed a month yet, correct?"

"Yes, sir."

"Right now, I don't have any assignments for you. If an opportunity does come along, I will let you know. Where is your desk in the office?"

I pointed towards the bench and he took a quick look.

"Oh, we cannot provide a chair and table for you at the moment because they are all occupied. However, you will have to come regularly and sit there for now. You will report to me, and I will approve your leave, allowances, everything."

Dogra sir had just begun to leave when the peon gestured for me to follow him.

"Sir… sir, I am ready for any kind of work…" I persisted.

"Be patient officer… wait for some time," Dogra sir replied calmly.

I thought it best not to argue lest I angered him and saluted again, "*Jai Hind*, sir!"

Meanwhile, a senior police officer came in and said that he needed an officer to manage traffic near the Legislative Assembly as the Chief Minister was to visit that day.

Dogra sir looked at me, and I spoke up before he could, "I will do it, sir." After which I got into the police van.

A day later, I showed my gratitude to the peon who had adroitly helped me put my case across to Dogra sir. He smiled a little and since then whenever he gets tea for his boss, he brings me a cup too.

❋❋❋

After my traffic control assignment, the days passed by without much change at the office. I sat on the same bench, day after day, the whole day. Occasionally, I got duty assignments usually dealing with managing traffic for VVIPs and politicians or making sure the arrangements in the Officers' Mess, for senior police officers, was ship-shape. I followed my orders, but I did not like the assignments much as I found them not on par with my capabilities.

One day, I was sent to the Police Club to look at how things were being managed. I was pleasantly surprised to see an Archery field after a long time. I picked up a bow, loaded an arrow on the stabilizer rod, pulled the bowstring, and released five arrows one after the other towards the target. To my shock, not a single one hit the bullseye. My normally excellent focus had deserted me, and it was glaringly obvious that my mind was in turmoil.

Chapter - 8

Present Day

"*Sahib*, no one will venture outside in this bad weather. Everyone has confined themselves to their cozy rooms." Ishwar climbs the steps and then walks into a corridor. He turns around sometimes while passing by a number of rooms, one after another. After leaving a few of them behind, Ishwar stops and says, "Everyone stays here itself, *Sahib*, but in separate rooms." Three of the rooms are placed adjacent to an attached washroom. Girdhari knocks on each room and waits for someone to answer.

"Shall I leave, *Sahib*?" Ishwar is eager to distance himself from the matter. *Indians are generally wary of the police as they have a negative view of them.* Girdhari nods and Ishwar moves away quickly.

※ ※ ※

The first person to answer the door is Saransh. He is surprised to see two policemen in front of him. He stands there in T-shirt and pajamas rubbing his eyes. Moments later, Ravi walks out of his room with messy hair, yawning widely. No response from the last room. Girdhari bangs on the door many times and shouts out, and is apparently ignored by the inhabitant, Ashok. Probably, he is not yet ready to leave his bed.

"This is the police… Open up!" Girdhari raises his voice. Ashok finally jumps out of bed and opens the door.

"Listen guys, we have come here to investigate a complaint we've received." Girdhari claps his palms loudly to draw the attention of the sleepy boys.

"What complaint…?" Saransh stammers.

"Is this the way to disturb someone?" Ravi interrupts.

"Hey, listen… hero…" Girdhari snaps his fingers twice and continues, "We are not happy to have come out in this weather either, and we are not here to play hide and seek with you."

"Let him finish, bro," Saransh interrupts.

Girdhari continues, "Varunika has filed a complaint saying that one of you has been troubling her."

"What do you mean? What kind of trouble?" Ashok asks.

Chandrika thinks of an appropriate answer and replies, "That is for us to figure out."

Ashok believes that the police are bothering them unnecessarily and musters up the confidence to speak, "Do you have a warrant to interrogate us?"

"This is just a routine enquiry for now and we are allowed to carry it out," Chandrika informs him politely.

On hearing that, Ashok too wants to distance himself from this useless business and pretends, "I have some urgent work at my office."

"All offices are closed today, don't you know? Please co-operate with us and everything will go smoothly and quickly."

"Ma'am, it appears you are harassing us unnecessarily. These two will stay back and answer your questions but I have to leave since I am late for work." Ashok smiles saucily and adds," Excuse me please."

Girdhari had enough of his callous behavior. He moves closer to Ashok and slaps him so hard, his five fingers leave a red imprint on Ashok's face. Ashok is caught off-guard and is in such shock that he freezes. Saransh finds it funny and wants to laugh but is afraid that the same fate might befall him. Ravi on the other hand swallows the lump in his throat and remains quiet.

Although Chandrika does not approve of what Girdhari did, she has no option but to keep quiet because she is in a hurry to reach Chandigarh and wants to finish the inquiry as soon as possible.

Chandrika crosses her arms and says, "Now, let's get on with the investigation. Everyone will sit in their respective rooms until we tell you what to do. Please hand over your mobile phones to Girdhari. No one will be allowed to make or receive phone calls during the interrogation, and you may neither meet or speak to each other or with anyone else."

"How long it will this take?" Ravi asks a little fearfully.

"Why? Do you have a date with your girlfriend? Just wait until we are done!" Girdhari says authoritatively.

"If you co-operate, we will finish as soon as possible. How smoothly the interrogation goes is up to you. *You* can make it easy on yourself or *we* will make it difficult." Chandrika signals to Saransh to go inside while Girdhari collects their mobile phones.

Saransh Patel's Story

"What is your name?" Girdhari asked me.

"Saransh Patel," I replied in an American accent. I was uncomfortable speaking in the presence of the local monster, Girdhari, who could slap anyone, anytime, without a warning. Despite my mother's warnings, I had gone forward with the project in India. Influenced by Hindi movies like Swadesh, I felt fortunate to visit India. In the movie, the hero, Mohan Bhargav, leaves his plush job at NASA and heads back to his village in India to help the locals. I was so inspired after watching that movie that I decided I must go back to explore my roots.

"NRI?" Chandrika asked me.

"Yes… I was ten years old when my parents moved to the Canada," I snapped out of my thoughts and replied.

Girdhari, the duffer, was unable to understand my accent and whispered, "Madam, is he speaking in some sort of different English?" I almost laughed at Girdhari's stupidity but suppressed the urge for obvious reasons.

"He lives in Canada," Chandrika replied and continued to make me feel comfortable while the duffer mumbled. "A deaf husband and a blind wife always make a happy couple."

Girdhari began wandering around the room picking up random things and staring at them as if he was seeing them for the first time in his life. Like Robert Patrick in the movie, Terminator 2, he occasionally picked up an object, scanned it, and then put it back with a perplexed expression. That gave me some comic relief. Chandrika observed this and disregarded it. There is always a good cop and bad cop on the team.

"So, what are you doing here?" she asked.

"I am a Phytologist and am here for a project."

"Can you speak Hindi too?" Girdhari closed an English magazine in which he had been trying to find 'special' pictures but gave up as he could not find anything interesting,

"Sure," I nodded. "Shoot!" Dumbass that he was, he looked at me weirdly and I quickly realized what I had said, and followed up with "I meant to say, ask me anything."

"Oh… okay…" The buffoon cleared his throat and asked, "You foreigners are rich, aren't you? Why are you staying at this place?"

I laughed a bit at how the image of all foreigners is distorted in India, "Nothing like that. Not all foreigners are rich. I belong to an ordinary family. My father runs a small store."

"Do you know Varunika, the one who stays at this resort?" Chandrika asked.

"Yeah… I mean, she is beautiful, attractive and charming."

"So, does that mean you can harass her?" Girdhari asked wrathfully.

"I never did!" I looked at Chandrika, controlled my nervousness, and replied defensively, "I didn't know that admiring beauty is an offence in India!"

"Turn on your mobile!" the ruffian commanded. I entered my secret pattern of dots. Girdhari checked out my phone but could not find anything. Then Chandrika took it and looked more keenly. She then asked for my laptop and password, which I refused to give.

Chandrika said politely, "Listen mister, if you do not co-operate with us the consequences can be pretty harsh for you. Just because I am polite, it doesn't mean that you can take me for granted."

"Let me call the embassy." I snatched my mobile and threatened them. I tried to go outside but had forgotten what had happened with Ashok a few minutes ago.

A sharp blow was in store for me. The room echoed first with the sound of the blow and then with my weeping. As soon as I recovered, I began typing the password. Chandrika scanned the desktop and clicked on the photo gallery.

"Hey, how much will you take to leave me alone?" I offered a bribe openly.

"Wait, English boy!!" For a second, Girdhari clamped down on my shoulder causing such anguish that I thought my bones would break.

"You cannot scrutinize my laptop like this." I tried to close my laptop but that brute pushed me back and I fell down from the chair.

Chandrika turned the laptop towards me and asked, "How did you get this picture?"

I glanced at the screen and replied, "She is a celebrity. Anyone can have her pictures."

"Hey, just answer what madam has asked."

I did not look at either and replied, "It has been downloaded from the internet. Is that a crime?"

"Don't act over-smart. We will figure out whether you downloaded it or not."

Girdhari then proceeded to open the cupboard and fling my clothes out.

"Stop it!!" I screamed as Girdhari pulled out a high-definition camera.

"I will examine the images on the memory card. So, are you going to tell us or should I insert the card in your laptop, to get the truth out?" Girdhari thundered.

I had been caught red-handed. I began crying loudly. Chandrika came by me and said, "Water?" I nodded and she gave me a glassful. With shaky hands, I sipped from it a few times. Then I said in a meek voice,

"The day was sunny and Varunika had just finished her bath. She came out of the bathroom and her long black curly hair was still wet. Her beauty overwhelmed my senses. Her nose stud was shining when the sunlight bounced off a tiny diamond. Her heart-shaped lips were a pretty shade of rosy-pink. She held a tiny lamb in her hands and was patting its white fur with her slender white fingers. It appeared as though, even the little lamb was proud to be in her beautiful hands.

The fact that it was in her hands made me feel as though the lamb was mocking me as all I could do was be jealous about it. In my life, I have never seen such a gorgeous woman. My heart palpitated faster with every glance. At one point I just felt like hugging her passionately and kissing every inch of her. I wanted to embrace her and lose myself in her sweet fragrance."

Girdhari cleared his throat and indicated with a head shake that I should control my emotions. Chandrika managed her feelings and remained expressionless.

After a few seconds, Girdhari mumbled, "Continue…"

"What?" I looked perplexed.

"What you were describing."

"I wanted to capture Varunika's million-watt smile desperately so I took a couple shots of her."

"Was she aware of it?"

"Maybe she was but that does not mean I created trouble for her," I tried to sound and look as innocent as possible.

"Listen, English boy, my job is to find out the truth. My seniors will come to investigate further."

"Ma'am…" I started to protest my innocence.

Chandrika stopped me and said, "Relax. You are not under arrest or anything. Just don't leave this city without informing the police. Where is your passport?"

I opened my pouch and took out my passport, credit and debit cards and other documents.

"Girdhari, click a picture of his passport," Chandrika ordered.

"Yes, madam." Girdhari photographed my passport with his mobile. He also took pictures of my debit and credit cards, including the CVV numbers. The dumb fellow did not realize that he was committing a breach of privacy by taking pictures of confidential data. Chandrika, in the meantime, had gone outside to check the network signal on her mobile.

"Hey, you can't take pictures of my cards and other confidential numbers," I protested.

The dummy ignored my dissent. Suddenly his interest was drawn to something else an imported packet of cigarettes. He swiftly grabbed the pack and put it in his pocket.

"Give me back that packet!"

Girdhari gestured for me to keep quiet by putting his index finger on his lips. I was worried about my credit card data and began hounding him to delete their images. Chandrika, finding no network on her mobile phone, returned to the room.

"What's the matter?"

"Ma'am, he took snapshots of my debit and credit cards," I whined like a schoolboy.

"What!? Girdhari, delete the pictures of his card details immediately from your phone." At first, Girdhari ignored Chandrika but when she stared him down, he slowly opened his phone and showed that the pictures had been deleted.

"See, English boy, there is nothing is here now. Happy?"

I did not respond and banged my door shut.

❧ ❧ ❧

Chapter - 9

"Madam, we have solved it. The English boy is the culprit. You must notify Dogra sir. Today is my son's birthday, so I have to leave early."

"Alright, I have to leave early as well."

"Sir told me to complete work as soon as possible. You are going to Chandigarh for your *Roka*, right? (*A ceremony where the bride and groom-to-be make a promise to each other that they will be married at a later date.*) Don't delay any longer; let's leave," Girdhari advised.

Chandrika ignored Girdhari's suggestion, "It will not take me much longer to finish up here as we have already got most of the answers."

"You proceed, I will join you in five minutes."

"Where are *you* going?"

Girdhari gestured that he wanted to have a smoke. "Madam, I need to warm myself in this biting cold," Girdhari makes up an excuse. Actually, he is dying for a few puffs of the imported cigarettes that he had acquired without spending a penny. *Anything free just doubles the pleasure.*

"Looks expensive, doesn't it?" Chandrika asks sarcastically.

"They're a gift, madam." Girdhari pauses, he doesn't think Chandrika will rumble him. Career-long, it has been his tried and tested method to get away with his ill-gotten gains. "My friend brought them from abroad," he adds with a smirk.

"Oh really!" Chandrika brushes him aside and moves on to knock on the next door. Girdhari sighs with relief.

Ravi Kumar's Story

"How long will this investigation go on for?" I asked a little sternly in the absence of Girdhari.

"Believe me, this is just a formality. May I come inside?"

I gave Chandrika an expectant look indicating *if I co-operate, I hope things will be sorted out quickly.* That was what I wanted most.

"Come in." I dragged a chair and Chandrika sat down.

"What is your name?" she asked.

"I am Ravi Kumar from Bihar and I work in a small private company from Jaipur which sells a local brand of water heaters and geysers. I have been here for almost five months now," I said quickly. I hoped we would be done before that *Banshira* (a sprit from Himachal folklore that changes into any form) came inside as well.

"Okay…" Chandrika wrote down the information in her diary and glanced around the room. She asked me to unlock my mobile and took a look at my picture gallery but found nothing of importance.

"Do you have a laptop or another computer?"

"No."

"Okay. How do you know Varunika?"

"She stays in this resort. I have seen her a few times. That's it." I was replying to every answer quickly to get myself out of this mess.

"That's it? Do you not find her attractive?"

"Of course, she is attractive and very beautiful, but I have never spoken to her."

"Madam, are we done here?" Girdhari came in and the smell of cigarette smoke filled the room.

"Almost… there is nothing suspicious in this room. I was waiting for you to open the cupboard and check it."

"Wait… wait!" Madam, you told me this is just a formality. Then, why are you asking him to search the cupboard?" I protested.

"It's part of our investigation. We must conduct a thorough search to ensure that you are clean."

The Banshira immediately moved to the cupboard, tried to open it, and found that it was locked.

"You cannot open it without a search warrant," I blustered.

The Banshira came near, stared at me for a moment, and then it happened again. He slapped me so hard that I could see whole galaxies of stars around me.

I controlled my tears before they rolled out. I gave him the key but before that I gave Chandrika a disgusted look. However, rather than accept her fault, she conveyed, *if you are honest, then there is no need to be afraid.* I turned my face away. Meanwhile, the *Banshira* searched the cupboard and found nothing except for my clothes, ties and belts. He took out a few pairs of clothes and tossed them aside.

"I had ironed those just yesterday," I complained.

That only made him angrier and he threw even more clothes on the floor.

I ground my teeth and cursed him under my breath.

The *Banshira* threw still more stuff from the almirah. At last, in the corner of a rack, he found an expensive bra in a transparent plastic pouch.

"Well, well…whom does this belong to?" the *Banshira* shouted. I tried to speak but no words came out of my stunned mouth.

Chandrika asked, "What do you know about this? Does it belong to your girlfriend?"

"Not girlfriend. I… I'm married," I stammered.

"You mean to say this is your wife's bra?" *Banshira* butted in.

"No… not my wife's."

"Oh, then whose? Do call girls visit you in this room?"

"Hey! I am not someone like that."

"So, whom does it belong to then? Speak up or else…" *Banshira* raised his arm.

"It is Varunika's bra," I blurted out, closing my eyes and bracing myself for another slap.

"Hmm… and how did you get hold of it?" Chandrika asked.

"I stole it from the laundry."

"What?!!! Why did you do that, you pervert?" the *Banshira* thundered.

"I know you will find it hard to believe, but the truth is that one of my friends paid me five thousand rupees to bring him her used bra. Initially, I refused, but then I thought that it is a good way to make some extra cash. During the pandemic, I was only paid half-salary. I needed the money desperately. At first, I purchased a new bra and handed it over to my friend but he figured out that it was not Varunika's."

"How did your friend know the difference?" Chandrika asked.

"He told me that she had visited his shop to buy an expensive bra, but as there is a very low demand for such bras in this area, he told her that it was out of stock. My friend knows the kind of bras she wears. So I had to acquire her original bra. I was about to deliver it today but due to the bad weather, I could not go out."

"Haha! Bad luck!" the *Banshira* smirked. For a few minutes, there was an uncomfortable silence. I covered my face and sat on the bed feeling ashamed of myself.

"Is there anything else you want to ask, madam?" the *Banshira* forcibly removed my hands from my face.

"No, we are done," Chandrika closed her diary.

The Banshira snapped his fingers to draw my attention, "Hey, mister… hello! We are leaving for now but don't you dare leave this place."

I did not respond and covered my face again.

๙๙๙

"What do you think madam? This guy is creepier than our English boy," Girdhari voices his concern before moving to Ashok's room.

"Do *you* think he was speaking the truth?" Chandrika asks.

"I don't know Madam. I just want to get our investigation over with and get home as soon as I can. Do we need to interrogate the third fellow too?"

"Yes, I think we will definitely get something from him as well. Let's see what secrets he has."

ॐ ॐ ॐ

Chapter – 10

Ashok Pathak's Story

Girdhari beat on my door and I opened it with fear written large on my face. My jaw was still smarting from the slap planted on my face earlier. I felt like I had gone partially deaf on one side, but who could I to complain to? They were the police and were capable of portraying a rope as a snake. I introduced myself.

❋ ❋ ❋

"So, have you come from Utter Pradesh to Shimla to work in this financial institute, as a Loan Officer?"

"Yes, ma'am."

"And is your full name Ashok Pathak?"

I nodded. "Yes, ma'am."

"Can I call your Manager to verify the information you have provided?"

My face turned pale immediately.

"What happened? Is there a problem?" The *Daitya* (Monster) asked in a harsh voice. He had figured out from my expression that something was amiss. I did not respond.

"What are you doing nowadays? I mean are you with the same company or have you quit?"

"Actually, ma'am, at the moment I am looking for a job."

"Why? Did you lose your job due to the pandemic or is there some other reason?"

I wanted to avoid answering the question and kept quiet. Girdhari did not want to waste time. He sat near me put one hand on my neck and whispered, "*Bhaiji* (Brother), if you do not tell us now, we will contact your boss tomorrow and he will spill the beans. So, it's better for you if you tell us what happened."

When I still did not reply, he showed me his hand, "Are you in the mood for one more?"

Helpless, I had no choice but to cooperate. "My colleague complained to my boss," I mumbled.

"What kind of complaint?" Chandrika was eager to know.

I continued to hesitate. Girdhari gripped my shoulder, shook me a few times and shouted. "Are you deaf? Madam just asked you what kind of complaint it was!"

His violent reaction scared me even more. "My colleague complained that I asked her to sleep with me." After saying that, I closed my eyes expecting another resounding slap.

"How dare you say such bullshit to a woman?" This was the first time Chandrika got angry.

"You bastard!" Girdhari grabbed me by my hair and struck me on my back with his fist. I shrieked in agony, "Aaaargh!"

"Have you slept with that girl before?"

"I thought Di… Div… Divya loved me as we used to go out on regular dates, to movies, dinner, etc., that's why I asked her." On hearing this, Girdhari let out a mischievous whistle.

"What about Varunika then?" Chandrika wanted to know. I repeated what I thought my friends might have said to her during their interrogations. Girdhari looked around my room and found that there were not many things lying around. I heaved a sigh of relief. Then, he headed to my drawer, opened it and took out a packet of condoms which he cunningly hid in his hand.

"Where is your wife?" His sudden politeness surprised me.

"She lives in her village with her parents and not has not been keeping well for the past one year," I thought revealing the plight of my wife might earn me some sympathy.

"What is wrong with her?" Chandrika asked.

"She has lymphosarcoma of the intestine."

"What!!!" *Daitya* tried unsuccessfully to repeat this.

Chandrika assisted him in pronouncing the illness. "Lym…pho…sar…coma of the intestine."

Daitya repeatedly murmured the name of the ailment. "I have heard this name somewhere before," he muttered, trying to appear knowledgeable.

"Rajesh Khanna had the illness," Chandrika clarified. Daitya continued to ponder about it, gently stroking his chin while trying to remember the title of the movie.

"Anand movie" Chandrika prompted helpfully.

"Ah, yes!" *Daitya* sparkled.

"Then to whom does this packet belong to?" *Daitya* was snorting through his laughter and was looking at me like he would slaughter me if I lied anymore.

I was startled into replying. "I know a couple of call girls and visit them at various hotels." Then shame overpowered me and I looked down.

In a fraction of a second, *Daitya* overturned the mattress that I usually slept on and found a heart-shaped envelope.

"What is this?" The letter inside it dangled from *Daitya*'s hand.

"Nothing… it is personal. May I have it back?" I requested, but crook that he is, he ignored me and began to read it.

"My beloved Varunika. I am a big fan of yours. Do you know which part of your body I think is the most beautiful…" he read and continued, mumbling under his breath so no one could hear him. In between, *Daitya kept looking up* at me but I dared not look back.

"What is this, *Bhaiji?*"

"A letter…" I faltered.

"This is not just a letter." *Daitya* grabbed me by my collar and added, "This is a *love* letter which clearly shows how sick you are."

Chandrika wanted to interrupt but kept quiet.

"Did you ever give her the letter?"

"I tried but I was not bold enough."

My collar was still in *Daitya's* grasp and I was writhing in pain. Finally, Chandrika intervened. "Leave him, Girdhariji."

I coughed for a minute and took a sip of water. Then I straightened my messy hair.

☙ ☙ ☙

Chandrika goes out to the passage and calls everyone for their final statements. Saransh, Ravi and Ashok stand in a line and act as if everything was alright and nothing had happened, but it was short-lived.

"Listen guys, we have completed our examination and. unfortunately, we have found evidence in all your rooms. This proves that each one of you had a motive to harass Varunika either on personal, emotional or other grounds. Since this is a sensitive issue, I will immediately submit a report to my seniors. They will decide what to do next. Meanwhile, no one should leave this town. If you must leave due to an emergency, please inform the nearest police station. I urge you not to discuss with each other, or with anybody else, what happened during the interrogations. Is that clear? Any questions?"

Everyone bent their heads and did not dare ask questions because they knew they were in trouble. They stood frozen in place.

Chandrika had their mobile numbers in her notes.

"Why all are you still standing here? Go back into your rooms and stay there." Girdhari admonished them for no reason.

* * *

Chapter – 11

Present Day | 11:00 AM | Day 1

"Girdhariji, do you think, what we did during the investigation, was right?" Chandrika is not happy with the way parts of the interrogation were conducted without official papers. It was only a complaint logged by a VVIP, and the police had begun working on the case without even meeting the alleged victim, Varunika. The sun is playing hide and seek between the clouds but the sunlight is not enough to warm anyone.

"Absolutely, madam." Girdhari assures her.

"We could have been more lenient with them."

"We were, madam." Girdhari says sarcastically. "You don't know what a show of power can sometimes achieve. Try it out some time and I am sure you will enjoy it. It's like a man-eating tiger. Once it has tasted human blood, it wants more and more."

Chandrika ignores him. She believes that what she had learned during training was the only truth. Girdhari inserts a key into the bike's ignition and just he is about to leave, a car stops abruptly in front of the gate. The driver steps out and opens the bonnet to check if something is wrong. While he is checking, some youngsters get out and immediately start creating a ruckus. A few of them begin playing with a beach ball while some others begin honking incessantly.

Chandrika and Girdhari notice the disturbance while talking to each other. Ishwar goes outside and shouts loudly for the youngsters to stop being a nuisance. In response, one of them hits the ball, which launches itself into an open compound and gets stuck in a small bush. He tries to get the ball but stops when he notices that the way is slick. He makes an effort to advance cautiously but skids. Ishwar gestures for him to stop and then calls for the security guard to throw the ball back outside.

A man comes out of a small room with long black beard and a moustache. He is wearing a mask on his face. He is coughing very hard. He takes a few seconds to locate the ball and hit it forcefully towards the gate, panting a little. The ball bounces several times and rolls out of the gate. In the meantime, the driver rectifies the problem and closes the bonnet. All the youngsters pile back into the car and it leaves. Just as soon as it had turned into a noisy fish market, the place falls silent.

Girdhari moves to start his bike when Chandrika asks him, "Which of the three boys do you think is guilty?"

"I think our English boy is the culprit. He is an NRI, and you know that he was eyeing Varunika from the way he described her beauty. What do you think, madam?"

"I am still confused. Dogra sir did not elaborate much. He just said, try to figure out who is troubling Varunika. He did not specify what kind of trouble Varunika is facing. Is she being harassed via phone calls, emails, messages or something else?"

Girdhari scratched his balding head and looked perplexed.

"Then, maybe Ashok is the culprit. We found the love letter and a condom packet among his stuff." Girdhari feels more relaxed after making this deduction.

"Why not Ravi? He too is only giving us half the truth. He may have stolen the bra for himself," Chandrika points out.

Girdhari has no answer. "Madam, the identification of the culprit should be left to Dogra sir."

Girdhari finally starts his bike, and the engine roars with its familiar phak-phak-phak!

Ishwar runs towards Girdhari and asks, *"Hazoor* tea… coffee… breakfast?"

"I am late."

Now Ishwar looks to Chandrika and asks, "Madam, would you like to have something?"

"No. I too must leave."

The sun has hidden itself again behind the clouds, which causes an increase in the cold rapidly.

Girdhari puts his bike into first gear. Before he can leave, Chandrika smiles and says, "Wish your son a Happy Birthday on my behalf. I will bring chocolates for him once I am back."

Girdhari nods and heads off. Once Girdhari has left, Ishwar insists, "Madam, give us an opportunity to serve you. It is such a cold day."

Chandrika asks, "Do you have a landline connection at the resort?"

"Yes, madam, we do. It's at the reception area."

Chandrika wants to report the day's interrogation and findings to Dogra from the resort itself. She goes to the reception, a small area with a thatched roof and a small kitchen, in front of which are a few chairs and tables where customers can eat. The kitchen is neat, the floor is spotless, and the wash basin is shiny and clean. The best feature is the beautiful panoramic view of the lush hills.

Chandrika pulls out one of the chairs and sits down. Ishwar is surprised that the chair didn't make a scratchy sound when it was dragged along. Chandrika blows hot air on her palms to warm them up. Ishwar opens a thermos flask and pours some tea into a white ceramic cup and serves it with some cookies. He stands nearby eagerly waiting for some positive feedback. Chandrika sips and praises the tea. On seeing Chandrika's happy face, Ishwar smiles too, and the upward ends of his salt-and-pepper moustache go up with his cheeks.

The police can never sit idle, they are always observant, and keep asking questions to understand their case. That is true of Chandrika as well.

"Nice kitchen, very neat and clean," Chandrika observes.

"*Jee* madam, we have to maintain it that way. Varunika madam likes it to be spotless."

Chandrika is impressed. She opens her diary and starts to take notes, "Why is the construction of this resort still incomplete and why is it still not fully functional? It seems that the condition of the rest of the place is not as good as the reception area. Why is it so?"

Ishwar takes a few minutes to compose his thoughts and says,

"Aryan *Sahib* started this resort just before the pandemic. He had ancestral land and he borrowed money from local lenders to develop it. Things, however, were impacted very badly by low tourist numbers. Covid-19 hit the business. *Sahib* faced huge losses and had to rent out a few rooms to town workers so that he could at least pay the utility bills –

electricity, water and so on. Apart from that, he has to pay the guard and cover my salary as well. *Sahib* assured me that things would be sorted out once the number of tourists went back to normal."

"Apart from these three guys, has anyone else stayed here earlier who has left now."

"No, madam. Only these three guys are staying here. Nobody is ready to stay so far on the outskirts."

"Okay. So, why did Varunika choose to stay here then?" The aromatic fumes of coriander and lemongrass wafting off the teacup helped relax Chandrika's mind.

"When Varunika madam shifted from Dalhousie to Shimla her husband bought a house two kilometers away. That house is being renovated, so they decided to stay here."

"In all, how many people stay at this resort?" Chandrika takes a bite of the cookie, and munches slowly, screening her mouth with a cupped palm so no one can see her chewing.

Ishwar starts to count on his fingers and speaks, "Ashok, Ravi and Saransh sir, Varunika madam and Hardik *Sahib*."

"Who is this, Hardik *Sahib*?" Chandrika interrupts him and places her cup gently on the table.

"Varunika madam's husband."

"Okay… anybody else?"

"Trisha madam."

"Who is she?"

"She checked in recently and is staying with Varunika madam."

Ishwar continues, "…and Shabnam and Kishan."

"Who are they?" Chandrika asks, noting everything down.

"Shabnam is madam's maid." Ishwar's expression changes as though he is proud to say Shabnam's name. Chandrika could see the joy on his face.

"So, she joins her in this cottage as well?"

"Yes, madam."

"Who is Kishan?"

"He is the watchman, madam." Ishwar's tone changes.

"Was he the one who threw the ball outside… What's the matter?"

"Madam, he is a TB patient. Keep away from him. Did you not see how he was coughing in the morning? Sometimes he removes his mask. I have often warned him not to be careless like that."

Chandrika stops writing, "Why is he still here?"

"I said the same thing to Aryan *Sahib* but he replied, *he is a very cheap resource. Sahib* pays him only five hundred rupees and I give him leftovers at noon and night. Once the guests check in, he is not here anymore."

"So, the total number of people staying at the resort now is nine?"

"Eight, madam."

"Eight?" Chandrika is confused.

"Hardik *Sahib* is busy with work, so he usually stays outside."

"Where is he today?"

"He left yesterday evening and has not returned yet." Chandrika nods but writes nine people in her notes.

"What about Ravi, Ashok and Saransh, how are they?"

"They are good. I do not talk to them much. They do come over for dinner on occasion. Otherwise, they mostly ask to be served in their rooms."

"How is their relationship?"

"Their interactions seem sporadic to me; they are mostly busy on their mobiles."

Ishwar puts Chandrika's cup in the sink and wipes the table with a dry cloth.

"Why is there no main gate in a resort this big?"

"We did have a main gate earlier but *Sahib* could not pay the vendor completely, he came and took away the gate. Money lenders were ready to confiscate this property." Ishwar lowers his voice and says, "That is the reason Aryan *Sahib* leased out this property to Hardik sir at zero cost. Now nobody comes to create trouble." Chandrika heaves a sigh of relief.

"Any CCTV?"

"Earlier, we had four cameras in madam's cottage but later, the guy who took the main gate uninstalled the cameras as well. Madam requests from time to time to get the cameras installed again but Aryan *Sahib* refuses. Varunika madam is rich but she tries to force Aryan *Sahib* by reiterating that it is for their safety. Finally, *Sahib* agreed to install one camera." Chandrika listens calmly.

"Why does that particular cottage look different from the others?"

The mixed vegetable soup is ready and Ishwar pours some into a thermos. "Aryan *Sahib* built that cottage for himself, to stay there with his family, but now Varunika madam lives there."

Chandrika looks at her watch again. She stands up, dons her cap, and asks, "Where is the phone?"

"Come this way, madam." Ishwar tilts his head to show her the way. They reach the reception area. A semi-circular wooden counter is there with a red phone on top of it. Behind it is written: 'Welcome to the Sky View Resort.'

Below the sign is a vacant black chair, covered with a thick layer of dust. Ishwar presses the button on the phone a couple of times to listen to the dial tone. However, all he gets is silence and sometimes static.

"What happened? Is the phone not working?" Chandrika stands in front of him with her hands folded across her torso.

"It was working fine this morning," Ishwar mumbles.

"Is there any other phone?" Chandrika turns impatient.

"We have another one but I do not know whether madam will allow us to use it."

Chandrika glares at Ishwar and that is enough for him to understand that he must provide an alternative. "Wait, madam." Ishwar runs to the kitchen and brings out the thermos, "Come with me. I have to take this soup to Varunika madam."

Chapter - 12

Ishwar and Chandrika stand at a porch surrounded by decorative green plants. A semi-circular, wooden, cherry-colored door is in front of them with a door knocker shaped like a lion's head which also matches the tiles on the floor. Chandrika looks at the CCTV camera above the door. Ishwar knocks on the door a few times and then waits. Shabnam opens the door a little. Chandrika is standing to the left of Ishwar and Shabnam is unable to see her. She asks very rudely *"Kya hai?"* (What is it?)

Ishwar gives her a broad smile and laughs unnecessarily. "Soup for madam."

"Did madam ask you bring it?"

"Yes, yesterday afternoon."

Shabnam opens door wide and prepares to take the flask from him. Ishwar smiles again and asks, "Is the landline working?"

"Yes… Trisha madam was speaking to someone just two minutes ago."

The pace of the conversation was slow enough to irritate even the most patient.

"Excuse me, where is the phone?" Chandrika interrupts impatiently.

Shabnam is surprised to see a police woman on their doorstep. She points speechlessly towards the table. This is the first time Chandrika makes a move without seeking permission. She uses the power of the uniform. Despite her brief acquaintance with it, the uniform has had a significant impact on Chandrika's thought processes without her even realizing it.

Shabnam disappears into a room.

☙ ☙ ☙

Chandrika finds herself in a different world. A big, round, sofa made of plush Italian leather is in the center of the room. The room has modest, pricey artworks that contribute to its affluent, high-end appearance. The floor is covered with an expensive red carpet. These and other little touches make the room appear luxurious.

Varunika and Hardik pose in a sizable, black, white and blue-toned photograph that captures the attention of everyone who enters. It portrays Hardik sitting on a chair with Varunika standing behind him, her hands over his shoulders running down in front of his neck till his chest. Small metallic lamps are arranged around the picture to grab the attention of guests. They both look happy and very much in love, *a couple made for each other*. On one side is a picture of Miss India, with Sixth Place written on it and to the left of that picture is another of Varunika holding a 'Model of the Year' trophy in her right hand.

Chandrika dials a number and waits for an answer. Meanwhile, she glances around the room admiring its décor.

"Hello, SP Dogra speaking."

"*Jai Hind,* sir," Chandrika begins providing an update, absentmindedly wrapping the spiral phone cord around her index figure.

"Chandrika, tell me, are you done?"

"Yes, sir."

"Send me the notes that you took during the interrogation."

"How shall I send them?"

"You're right, everything is down. Go to the office and hand them over to Constable Verma. He knows my fax number. One thing… be careful when you hand him the notes. Use an alias and once done, take back all the documents."

"Certainly, sir."

"After that you are free to go."

Chandrika is relieved and replies, "Thank you, sir'. She takes out a pen, strikes out the names of the suspects and replaces them with aliases. Chandrika does all this bending over the table where she called her boss from. She straightens up massaging her stiff neck and looks around. She notices that she is alone. The wall clock reads 12:00. The ticking and tocking of the clock seems to say: *Chandrika, move faster.*

ॐ ॐ ॐ

Before leaving, Chandrika feels the need to inform someone. She looks towards the corridor, the roof and walls of which are constructed in glass hued purple from the vines covering it on the outside. She walks around and finds that all doors are closed except for a light-green one that is slightly open with some light leaking through it. Chandrika thinks that someone might be inside and knocks on the door. It slides open a little.

Looking in, she is stunned by the sight. The dressing table is packed with different brands of makeup and cosmetics, ranging from the expensive to the super exclusive. There is parlor equipment of so many kinds that it would boggle the imagination of a common person.

A big poster of Varunika hangs on the wall, in which she appears fresh and lively. Chandrika sits down on a recliner and looks at the mirror. She clicks a button and all the bulbs, around the edges of the mirror come on. She picks up one item after another, nail paints of different colors, eyeliners, lotions and many more. She opens a container of cream and takes a whiff from it. She holds different kinds of combs in her hand and wonders what they are for.

Almost 15 minutes pass this way with Chandrika lost in a different world. Suddenly the room door opens briefly and a beautiful woman enters. She is none other than Varunika in a white bathrobe. Her hair is wet and her hands are tucked into the front pockets of her robe. She is startled to see a stranger in the room and screams.

For a moment, Chandrika is taken aback too and quickly puts the nail paint down. "Ma'am, I was only looking at this stuff. I did not use anything."

Varunika is frozen where she is. Trisha, who is following her with a glass of white wine, hears the scream and quickly enters the room. Chandrika is nervous, and swiftly begins to introduce herself. Varunika regains her composure in a moment but is still not listening to Chandrika. She tightens her bathrobe and takes a deep breath. Trisha gives Varunika an assuring pat signifying *everything is okay.*

"Ma'am, I was just looking…" Chandrika stammers, embarrassed at being caught red-handed. There is an awkward silence in the room and Chandrika uses that time to observe Varunika from the side, as a devotee would their idol. With glowing skin, deep brown eyes, bouncy hair, heart-shaped lips, Varunika is the perfect blend of beauty and allure. No one can ignore her dazzling glamour.

Even though Varunika is only about 35 years old, she looks at least 8-10 years younger. Far younger and more beautiful than Saransh had described. After a couple of minutes, Trisha breaks the ice and gives the glass of wine to Varunika.

"Ma'am, did you like yesterday's pictures, the ones which we clicked in morning?" she asks.

Varunika does not reply as she considers it the wrong time and place to discuss her personal or professional matters in front of Chandrika. She continues to sip her wine quietly. Trisha understands and gives Chandrika a look conveying, *it's time to leave and give ma'am some privacy.*

Chandrika clears her throat, "Ma'am, I have completed my interrogation of the alleged suspects and came here to inform Dogra sir of the progress. I did not intend to intrude but this is the only operational landline in the resort."

Varunika notices Chandrika staring at her swallow-like eyes. She quickly opens a cupboard, takes out sunglasses to match her attire, and immediately covers her eyes.

Chandrika before leaving asks, "Ma'am, I have a question. How exactly did the alleged suspects harass you?"

Varunika shrugs and expresses an interest in hearing more. Chandrika clarifies, "I mean, how does the culprit trouble you? By phone, on social media, or by any other means?"

Varunika still does not reply. She finishes the remaining wine and gives the empty glass to Trisha.

"SP Dogra told me you have a *Roka* ceremony to attend tomorrow," Varunika says in a soft voice, changing the topic.

"Yes, ma'am." Chandrika is happy that a celebrity is enquiring about her engagement function.

"Is it an arranged marriage or is it love?"

"Arranged, ma'am. My parents met him first and now I will get to meet him."

"That is good. You know, in love marriages, the expectations are high on both sides."

"What about you ma'am? Did you have an arranged marriage or was it love?"

Varunika smirks, "You are the one in the police, why don't you tell me?"

"I believe it was a love marriage."

Varunika nods slowly and confirms it. Trisha smiles. Chandrika looks at her and a smile forms on her face for a moment. She observes, however, that Varunika seemed to be under some sort of pressure.

"So you have a special day tomorrow, but look at your skin… it looks so rough and tired, no glow at all. Did you not find a good beauty parlor, at least for a touchup?" Varunika sits down and relaxes.

Chandrika touches her face self-consciously and replies, "I did go to a parlor but it was their very products that caused an allergic reaction on my skin."

"Trisha, can you take care of her? I must leave now," Varunika says, getting to her feet.

"Sure, ma'am."

Varunika takes Trisha aside and whispers some instructions. She says to Chandrika, "By the way, I forgot to introduce Trisha. Trisha works in the glamour industry with Bollywood. She is a stylist who provides beauty treatments as well as costume design services for celebrities. She will be with me for the next six months to help me complete my projects. Oh, and one more thing, she also takes good photographs. If you don't mind, I have asked her to help you out."

Chandrika is amazed and delighted at this unexpected development after the painful events of the past six months. How tiring life had been and now, finally, God was being very kind to her.

❦ ❦ ❦

Once Varunika leaves, Trisha gets started. She takes out her laptop, connects a rod to one of the ports and moves it around Chandrika's skin to analyze its tone and texture. As she does that, many different graphs are simultaneously generated on the laptop. Then she begins her analysis.

"You are right, your skin is sensitive and needs extra care and nourishment. It seems you have applied too many different products on your face due to which your skin has turned even more sensitive. Are you aware of that?"

Chandrika shook her head.

Trisha then takes out a yellow bathrobe from the wardrobe and gives it to her. Chandrika runs her hand on its surface and finds it to be very soft. She is, however, unsure what to do with it. Trisha points to the washroom and indicates that Chandrika must change into the bathrobe.

Chandrika enters the bathroom quietly and emerges in a few minutes. She sits facing a mirror but avoids looking at herself. Trisha begins her work. At first, she arranges all the required cosmetics on the table and then begins to apply them on Chandrika.

"Has your hair always been parted on the left?" Trisha asks after she finishes washing Chandrika's hair.

Chandrika nods.

"Well, we are going to change that to a Princess hairstyle with burgundy-colored highlights." Chandrika wisely decides not to ask any questions as she believes that she is in the good hands of one of the best beauticians. Instead, she closes her eyes and enjoys the light music that is playing in the background. It takes around two hours for the makeover to be completed.

*** *** ***

"Now look at yourself in the mirror."

Chandrika turns towards the mirror. For a second, she cannot believe her own reflection. Chandrika touches scar which has hidden by good make up. The new look is spellbinding. She is so transfixed by her image that Trisha has to snap her fingers to get her attention.

"Shall we go now?"

Chandrika is jolted out of her trance and replies, "Yes." She stands up and moves to the washroom.

"Wait, wait! First let's go and meet Varunika ma'am. She has planned something more for you."

While they are walking through the corridor, Trisha asks her, "Do you like your new look?"

Chandrika nods shyly.

"Do not wash your face with soap. Use this facewash and do not rub your face too hard for the next three days."

They enter the dining room where Varunika, dressed in black casuals, is standing on the balcony sipping red wine.

"Ma'am…" Trisha calls out, Varunika does not respond. She is lost in her own world. Trisha calls out again, this time a little louder, "Ma'am!!" Varunika turns around and sees them. She adjusts her glasses.

She glances at Chandrika and says, "You look so pretty. For a moment, I could not recognize you."

Chandrika smiles shyly.

Varunika gestures for Chandrika to take a seat. Trisha also sits beside her.

Chandrika says, "Ma'am, Trisha says you have something more planned but I do not have much time. I have to go home, pick up my backpack, and reach the Army depot. It is ten kilometers from there. From there, I must catch the bus that goes to Chandigarh."

"So, when will you reach?"

"Earlier, I had planned to get there by lunchtime, now it looks like it will be dinnertime before I reach. We have planned a small get-together with my fiancé's family to complete some formalities."

"Oh, and you are late because of my complaint, right?"

"No ma'am, just doing my duty."

"I know… and you have performed it excellently. Dogra called me and expressed his admiration for your work. He also assured me that the culprit, or culprits, will be caught soon."

"Thank you, ma'am."

"What clothes are you planning to wear for your ceremony?"

Chandrika opens the photo gallery in her mobile and shows her a few pictures. "Which of these do you feel is good?"

"Have you had your lunch?" Varunika interrupts.

"I will have it later."

"That's not okay! You must never skip a meal." Varunika calls Shabnam and asks her to arrange for lunch. She then takes a few small sips of wine. Shabnam quickly sets the table and places some multigrain bread rolls, sautéed green vegetables, *chapatis*, roast beans, brown rice, fruits and yoghurt on the table.

"Trisha, what would you like to have?"

Trisha goes for the sautéed vegetables first, then picks up a chapati and serves herself some roasted beans.

"What about you, Chandrika?"

"Ma'am, I'll serve myself." Chandrika scoops up some brown rice with yoghurt and takes a helping of fruits from a bowl.

Meanwhile, Varunika finishes her glass of wine and pours herself another. Shabnam asks, "Ma'am, do you want anything else?"

Varunika replies, "The boiled vegetables and a bread roll are enough for me."

For a while, the only the sound in the room is that of cutlery clinking on dinner plates. Chandrika decides to break the ice as she thinks that this is the best opportunity to pursue her secret desire. "Ma'am, do you think I can become a model?"

Trisha stops chewing for a moment, while Varunika scans Chandrika from top to bottom. She says, "Of course, you can become a model. You have the height, long hair and nice body language. The problem I see is with your rough skin and…"

Varunika stops for a moment and Chandrika knows what's coming next. "… that scar on your chin. Am I right Trisha?"

"Yes, ma'am. You are absolutely right." Trisha places her fork on her plate and leans back on her chair.

Chandrika sees her dreams being shattered once more but Varunika adds, "That is not so much of a concern though. You must undergo a skin-whitening treatment which will transform your look completely. The scar can be taken care of after minor cosmetic surgery."

"Are these procedures and treatments expensive?" Chandrika asks, displaying her naivete.

"Yes, my dear. All these are done abroad. But don't worry. I have some good contacts." Varunika takes a few more sips of wine.

"What is the next step?" Chandrika is eager now.

"Next? You will have to participate in the Miss Shimla contest next year and win the crown," Trisha interjects, displaying her knowledge on the topic. Varunika gives her a thumbs up while Chandrika wonders: *Is it that simple?*

"After that?" Chandrika feels a surge of excitement from within but does not let it show on her face. She knows from her past experiences that dreams are very fragile and if broken, they cause immense unhappiness, emotionally and psychologically.

"If you are successful, you will probably be offered endorsement deals from various companies to promote their products and that will help you establish a footing in the industry. But remember, this is the Miss Shimla contest and not Mrs. Shimla," Trisha winks mischievously.

The human brain works very fast and is always on the lookout for different ways to achieve its goal. Chandrika's brain too is already ready with a scheme, *I will just get engaged, and put off the wedding until I win the Miss Shimla contest.*

❧ ❧ ❧

Shabnam returns and clears away the lunch. Varunika stands up and instructs Chandrika to follow her. She enters a room, switches on the lights, and pushes open the sliding door of the wardrobe. Chandrika is wonderstruck at the huge collection of clothes, footwear and bags, each one more expensive and luxurious than the next. Varunika selects two dresses and tells her to try them on, one after the other. She also takes out matching pairs of footwear and purses. Chandrika is hesitant as she feels completely out of place in this opulence.

"What is the matter?"

"Nothing." Chandrika shakes her head and adds, "These dresses are too expensive."

"So what? Consider them a gift. Go, change."

Chandrika heads off and returns after ten minutes. The first words out of Trisha's mouth are, "Wow! Gorgeous! You look beautiful."

"Trisha, look at her eyebrows, though. They need a trim."

"They have already been tweezed, ma'am."

"Not enough. Trim them so they look sleeker."

Trisha is unsure how much more to trim and stands perplexed. Varunika takes the tweezer in her hand and attempts it herself.

"How about that?"

"Perfect, ma'am"

Chandrika looks at herself in the mirror once again.

"See how small changes can make big improvements in a person's appearance?" Varunika says and finishes her wine. "Well, I am a bit tipsy now. Trisha, take care of the rest."

"Thanks, ma'am," Chandrika says. Varunika takes Trisha aside once again and whispers more instructions.

"It is alright." Varunika replies without looking at Chandrika and goes to her bedroom. She, however, appears to be hiding something, judging from the tension on her face.

જ જ જ

Trisha takes out an expensive camera and clicks a few pictures of Chandrika. She asks Chandrika to pose in different ways. She is, however, not happy with the results. Chandrika poses stiffly and appears nervous.

"Look, Chandrika, once you are on the ramp, you must forget all your inhibitions. Remember, if you feel awkward about yourself it will show in your actions and attitude, and no amount of make-up or snazzy attire will be able to hide it. Think that you are the most good-looking person in the world. Now, let us see that confidence."

Trisha then clicks some more pictures and shows Chandrika the difference in them from the previous set. She is happy that her words have encouraged Chandrika to shed her shyness and appear more confident. She then transfers the images to Chandrika's mobile.

"Do you have a Facebook account?"

"I am on WhatsApp in a couple of groups including an animal welfare group."

"Show me your Display Picture."

Chandrika opens her WhatsApp account which has a picture of a small puppy. Trisha laughs and says, "Change your DP." Chandrika nods and promises that she will do it later.

Chandrika is sure that if she had visited a posh parlor for these treatments, she would have had to sacrifice nine months of her salary.

Chapter - 13

Trisha calls Shabnam and asks, "Has Ramdeen come?"

"Yes, madam. He came two hours ago and is waiting in the car."

"Good. Let's move. Chandrika, you are already late."

A white SUV is parked outside. A 56-year-old driver in a white uniform is taking a nap in the back seat. Trisha knocks on the door and shouts, "Ramdeen… Ramdeen!" He snaps out of his nap and exits the car.

"Yes, madam."

"Drop this ma'am wherever she wants to go."

Chandrika looks at Ramdeen and says, "Army Depot."

"The one which is outside the city?"

"Yes."

Ramdeen is not in a mood to go anywhere, especially in the inclement weather. Trisha looks at him and says, "No, not the Army Depot. Drop her in Chandigarh."

Ramdeen is confused about whom to listen to. He now feels that the Army Depot is a better option than going all the way to Chandigarh. Chandrika wants to decline the offer but before she can say anything, Trisha says, "Chandrika, you will get unnecessarily tired. And the weather is not very good either. This vehicle has a nice heating system which will ensure a comfortable journey."

"What about Varunika ma'am?" Ramdeen says, hoping to avoid the long journey.

"Don't worry about that. Ma'am has nothing planned for today. If required, we have another four-wheeler that I can take her out in."

Chandrika is finally persuaded and is glad to have such a comfortable option for her journey. The SUV has just started up when Chandrika realizes that she has forgotten her uniform in the washroom. Trisha immediately calls Shabnam and asks her to fetch it quickly. Shabnam folds it, places it in a handbag, and gives it to Chandrika.

"Where do we have to go, madam?" Ramdeen asks softly.

"Police Headquarters."

Ramdeen is confused at being presented with a third option but follows her instructions without saying anything more. Chandrika updates the notes in her diary with one more name, Ramdeen.

The roads are relatively empty and their journey is smooth and uneventful. Chandrika wants to update her DP on WhatsApp, but the internet is down so no one can see her new avatar. She is happy though, and smiles thinking about the events of the day. Given her past experiences, she never though a day would come when she would actually be viewed as beautiful. She is excited to see what the future has in store for her.

Ramdeen steers the car into a compound and reminds her, "Madam, we have reached." Chandrika is lost in a dream world and does not pay attention.

Ramdeen repeats a little louder, "Madam, the Police Headquarters."

"Huh?" Chandrika leaves her thoughts behind, opens the door and quickly heads inside. Curious about her behavior, Ramdeen decides to follow her. She crosses the corridor, heading for a room where a constable is sitting outside watching something on his mobile. Ramdeen moves closer as well. Chandrika moves past the constable, then reverses her steps.

"Mohan!" she says in a loud assertive voice. Mohan does not pay heed as he is glued to the mobile screen that has a beautiful woman on it. However, the very next moment, he spots Chandrika in the corner of his eye and realizes who she is. He stands up and salutes her quickly, "Sorry, madam. I did not recognize you. This is the first I am seeing you in this attire."

Ramdeen gets back to his seat and mumbles, "*Arrey, baap rey! Yeh toh police main hai (Oh my! She is in the police)*."

Chandrika calms down and turns polite. She gives the constable her diary and says, "Fax these pages to Dogra sir."

"Yes, madam." Chandrika follows him. For the first time, there is an unusual confidence in her gait. Mohan switches on the fax machine to send the files.

"Done?" Chandrika asks.

"Yes, madam… just one more thing… please do not complain to sir," Mohan pleads.

"Alright, but be careful and more attentive next time. "

"*Jee*, madam."

Ramdeen's behavior has also turned polite. "Where do you want to go next, madam?"

"Rivoli Road."

☙☙☙

Chapter – 14

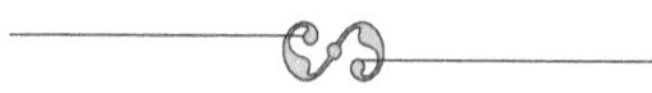

"Where is my key?" Chandrika mumbles and searches for the key in her pocket. Suddenly she remembers, Aha! It must have fallen out when Shabnam handed her the uniform. Or it was in the cottage's washroom where she changed her clothes. *Hmm, it's alright. I have a spare key at my neighbor's house.* That thought lends some relief to Chandrika.

Chandrika rings the doorbell. Ting, Tong!

For a few seconds, there is no response and she gets impatient. She wants to reach Chandigarh at least in time for dinner. Chandrika presses the button again and waits. An elderly person calls out from the other side, "Coming… wait!"

Dadwal Uncle opens the door and asks, "Yes?"

Chandrika is surprised, "Don't you recognize me, uncle?"

Uncle takes some time and replies, "Oh, Chandrika! Sorry I could not recognize you at all. You look so beautiful. Come… come inside."

"Uncle, I have misplaced my house key and need the spare one from you."

Uncle ponders for a moment. Meanwhile, someone calls out from inside, "Who is at the door? Who are you talking to?"

Usually, in cold places, there is a small alcove by the door where people hang their overcoats. Dadwal uncle goes inside.

"It's Chandrika," Uncle lowers his voice.

"Oh, that ugly girl. Get rid of her quickly. I don't consider her *Himachali*."

Chandrika can clearly hear the voice and feels quite embarrassed.

Dadwal aunty asks again, "Has she left or not?"

Chandrika feels hurt and angry at the same time. She wants to slap Dadwal Aunty silly but that would only work against her. The people would certainly support Mrs. Dadwal.

She felt like running away but decides to stay and show aunty how her appearance has changed.

Before Aunty can say anything inappropriate again, Uncle decides to control her fiery tongue. He puts a finger on his lips to signify that aunty should keep silent and says, "She is with me."

Uncle moves out of the way and aunty finally catches a glimpse of Chandrika. She cannot believe that the beautiful woman behind her husband is Chandrika. She adjusts her spectacles and looks at Chandrika again. The shock is evident on her face.

Their daughter, Vimi, who is sitting on a sofa, turns her face towards Chandrika and shrieks, "Chandrika *Didi*! You look so beautiful. What is this magic that *jijaji* (brother-in-law) has performed on you? And why have you still not shared his picture with us?"

Chandrika tucks a lock of hair behind her ear and smiles coyly. Vimi takes her to the sofa and looks at her dress. "Even your dress is so pretty. Which shop is it from? How much did it cost?"

Chandrika, has no idea how to answer. She shows Vimi the tag which she had removed. Vimi squeals in excitement. "Mom, it is designed by Shilpa Dhariwal, the designer."

Vimi looks at her mother, who mumbles, "Oh, really! Then it must be expensive. What does it cost?"

"Let me check it out," Vimi replies and flips the tag around. She sees that the printed price says Rs. 70,000. Uncle asks if Chandrika would like some tea but she refuses.

Aunty, the opportunist, loses no time in asking, "Chandrika, what is your salary like?"

Chandrika decides that it is better to leave. Her snub does not go down well with Aunty, and she shoots off, "Most police officers are corrupt. They take bribes, either directly or indirectly, Don't they?" Vimi, who is just 16 years old does not understand the reference.

Uncle whispers to his wife, "For God's sake, lower your voice!"

"I don't care whoever is there!" Aunty is a little louder than before.

Uncle quickly hands over the key to Chandrika, who controls her anger. He is ashamed of his wife's behavior and avoids her eyes. Chandrika leaves the place without saying anything.

ॐ ॐ ॐ

"Mom, I am just leaving," Chandrika tells her mother sternly. The harsh tone of her voice is a direct result of the treatment she received from Dadwal Aunty.

"Chandrika, you are so careless. Daksha will be leaving tomorrow for higher studies and will not return for another year. Don't you understand that we have managed to find a suitable match for you with great difficulty?"

"I know, but how can you say he is a suitable match? He stutters while speaking," Chandrika mumbles.

"Oh yeah? Do you think some handsome prince will come along riding on his horse to rescue you?"

"Mom, I was stuck on a case," Chandrika interrupts her. "I will get there on time, don't worry." Chandrika's voice shows her vulnerability.

"This morning, I told you to bring my sari. Did you pack it in your bag?"

"Yes, Mom..."

"...but you did not listen to what else I needed."

"What?" Chandrika is in no mood to continue the conversation.

"Chintu has forgotten his sharpeners when we left, bring those too."

Chandrika looks at her study table, opens a zipper pouch and puts them in the bag.

"Anything else?"

"Do you have the hotel's address?"

"Yes, Mom. I will reach on time," Chandrika replies as though she has surrendered to the situation.

"For God's sake, lower the TV volume. You have been watching the same breaking news again and again," her mom says irritably.

"What news is Papa watching?" Chandrika is curious.

"Someone's husband has been murdered."

"Murdered? Whose husband?" Chandrika is annoyed at receiving incomplete information.

Phoola calls out to her husband while Chandrika waits on the phone. "Varu... Varunika? Oh, that famous model! Her husband is the son of Home Secretary Mr. Dhawan... last night?"

"What?? Mom, can you repeat that?"

"Are you deaf? Varunika's husband..." What Phoola says after that is inaudible. Chandrika hangs up the phone and immediately calls her boss.

☙ ☙ ☙

" Hello, sir..."

"What's the matter? Are you still in Shimla?"

"Sir, you hid the information about Varunika's husband's death from me."

Dogra does not reply. Chandrika continues, "Was Varunika aware of it? Was the investigation I did merely a formality?" Chandrika is angry but she knows who she is talking to so she holds back. Although she keeps her tone polite her pain is evident.

Dogra flares up, "Listen, Chandrika, I am your boss and I don't have to answer your questions."

"I am sorry, sir," Chandrika lowers her voice.

"This is not an easy puzzle. We wanted to keep this case under wraps till tomorrow afternoon, but someone has leaked the info to the media, and now every channel is broadcasting it as breaking news. There is a great deal of stress. We need to catch the culprit by tomorrow morning, otherwise the Chief Minister of the State will come under pressure to resign. Anyway, since you have already been released from this case, you may head off for your previous commitment. I will find someone else."

In the heat of the moment, Chandrika is unable to walk the fine line between dreams and ambition. Dreams are fragile but ambition makes a person selfish. She decides to stay on and work on the case. Additionally, she desires a closer relationship with Varunika for which she is ready to sacrifice her principles.

"Is it okay if I continue on this case, sir?"

Dogra remains quiet for a moment and Chandrika repeats the question.

"Hmm… uhhh… okay, you can continue to work on the case on one condition—you cannot leave town for the next few weeks, regardless of how dire your situation is."

"Yes, sir. I understand."

"You must assure me that you will follow the rules of the game. I do not want a repetition of your behavior from your previous case."

"I will make sure that it doesn't happen, sir."

"Alright then, let me explain it to you. Currently, we have a hung legislative assembly, and the ruling party is supported by two other parties, the Vikas Dal and Awam ki Shakti. Everything went well initially but later, differences sprung up between the ruling party and the Vikas Dal. The Vikas Dal threatened to withdraw their support and are looking for a good excuse to do so.

Hardik was murdered in Kalaka, which comes under Haryana, where the Vikas Dal enjoys a complete majority. That is the opportunity they want to cash in on. If the Haryana police uncovers a political angle behind the murder, then the Chief Minister will be forced to resign. You know, these bigwig politicians have many skeletons in their closets. So, when they come to power, the opposition is constantly looking for opportunities to dig them out.

Last night, when I informed Varunika about her husband's death, she sobbed a lot. When I asked if she suspected anyone, she said it could be one of the three guys living at the resort.

"Does she have a solid reason to suspect them?"

"According to her, since she has a large fan following, she maintains multiple mobile numbers. Out of those, she has set one aside for fan communication. She is very active on social media and other platforms, updating her followers on her new shoots and other activities. Sometimes she communicates with them over WhatsApp too.

One day, when she connected with a fan, he told her about how he knew her daily routine: when she woke up, what she ate, what she wore, where she went…everything. That put her under a lot of stress because she felt that that fan was actually a stalker.

The resort is built on a slope. It is in a remote location with nothing but short grass in the surrounding area. She tried to monitor the surroundings for the stalker but could not find him. As time went by, she forgot about it. All of a sudden, a day came when he called and threatened to kill Hardik. No one knows why perhaps obsession or jealousy. And now Hardik is dead. Coincidence? I think not."

"Do we have that number under surveillance?" Chandrika starts with basic questions.

"The mobile number is under surveillance but it has not been active since yesterday morning. We checked out the Aadhar card which was submitted with the number as well. It turned out to be fake. Before the phone turned off, the last known location was the resort or its surroundings."

"Sir, do we have any other details about the murder?"

"We have conducted an initial investigation and it appears that only one person is involved. The autopsy report will be issued after some time. I have already sent four constables to keep a watch at the resort. I think this much information is enough for you to go on."

"Yes, sir."

"Go in plainclothes as a police uniform may tip off the media. Ask Girdhari to join you. If he is unable to manage, inform me, I will call a suitable Head Constable for you."

"Yes, sir." Chandrika hangs up and unpacks her belongings. She leaves Varunika's dress on, covering it with a thick black overcoat to protect her from icy winds.

�❅❅❅

Chapter – 15

"Take me back to the resort." Chandrika is in a hurry.

"Not Chandigarh?" Ramdeen is happy.

Chandrika has not yet made up her mind about calling Girdhari. She knows it is his son's birthday and thinks she can handle the interrogation herself by being a bit sterner. She still needs someone who can help her find out who the culprit is, at any cost.

"The phone network is up now, madam. Life is hell without mobiles nowadays. You feel isolated in this world," Ramdeen says.

"Huh?" Chandrika's thought process is interrupted. She finally decides to call Girdhari.

"Hello, madam. I'm surprised to receive your call. I didn't know the phone network was up."

"Girdhariji, can you do me a favor?"

"Yes, tell me, madam."

"Can you come to the Sky View Resort?"

"Oh, are you not in Chandigarh?"

"No, I am still in Shimla."

"What happened?"

Chandrika covers her mouth and speaks softly, "Open Google and type Varunika."

Ramdeen looks at Chandrika through the rearview mirror in an attempt to figure out what is going on.

"Oh my God! I can't believe it." Girdhari is shocked after reading news of Hardik's murder. A few minutes later, he calls back.

"Madam can you call another head constable? You know it's my son's birthday and I'm quite busy here."

"Girdhariji, it is around 5:00 PM and I think we will be able to figure out the culprit within two to three hours. You may leave by 8:00 PM. Anyway, your guests will arrive only around 7:00 PM."

Girdhari thinks about it.

"Girdhariji this is a high-profile case. If things go well, you will definitely be promoted to SI."

Girdhari is in a dilemma about which to choose: his kid's birthday or an opportunity for a promotion. Then a thought moves through his mind: *if I get promoted to SI, next year I can celebrate my son's birthday in a big hotel.*

"What are you thinking about Girdhariji? Shall I call someone else?"

"I'll come, madam"

Ramdeen guesses from Chandrika's mood that something wrong has happened. He ignores it thinking it best not to interfere with police work. Meanwhile, Chandrika sends the mobile numbers of all three suspects to the surveillance team to trace their locations at the time of the murder.

❦ ❦ ❦

A constable posted there stops the approaching vehicle as it nears the resort. Chandrika gets out and introduces herself, "SI Chandrika."

"*Jai Hind, madam.*" The four constables salute Chandrika.

Now Ramdeen's doubts become even stronger. *Something bad has transpired here.* He quietly parks his vehicle.

❦ ❦ ❦

The resort's atmosphere is as silent as can be. After exiting the vehicle, Chandrika immediately takes her team through the corridor and orders them to knock on the doors. All three occupants open their room doors and stand quietly. Chandrika gestures to one of the constables to collect their mobiles and directs another to seize their laptops and other electronic gadgets. They are then made informed about the murder. They instantly realize they are in deep trouble.

Just then, Girdhari arrives and joins Chandrika.

Ashok shows some courage, "What is going on?"

"You are now murder suspects. Any one of you could be the culprit," Chandrika replies firmly.

"I did not do anything. I am a vegetarian," Saransh stammers.

"Do you have a warrant or will this too be like the last interrogation?" Ravi jumps in, but one look from Girdhari is enough to shut them up.

"Listen guys, if you co-operate with us we will make sure that the culprit is caught and punished. Otherwise, you know how the police do their job," Girdhari warns.

"Sit in your rooms and do not come outside until we call you." Chandrika deputes two constables to keep an eye on the suspects.

Chandrika and Girdhari walk towards Varunika's cottage. On the way, she fills him in on what Dogra told her.

"Girdhariji, first let me ask Varunika a few questions."

"Shall I come in?"

"No, I will question her alone. Meanwhile, get the locations and call logs of all the suspects."

"Okay," Girdhari agrees reluctantly.

"Dogra sir has ordered us to wear civilian clothes while interrogating."

Ishwar sees Chandrika and comes out crying, "What happened? *Sahib* was well when he left yesterday evening. What is this running on the News?"

"We are investigating the matter. Co-operate with us."

Ishwar wipes his tears on his sweater's sleeves. Girdhari, in the meantime roams around the resort looking for clues.

❦ ❦ ❦

Chandrika knocks on the door and Shabnam opens it. She too is sobbing.

"Where is madam?" Chandrika asks politely.

"She is sleeping in the upper room," Shabnam replies, hiccupping between sobs.

"Have some water," Chandrika suggests kindly.

Before going upstairs, she glances at the beautiful picture of the happy husband and wife and thinks to herself, *there's nothing left now; everything is ruined.*

On the first floor, Trisha is sitting on a sofa outside the bedroom with her eyes closed. Her expression is miserable, no doubt after hearing the news. Chandrika shakes her a bit.

"Huh? Oh, Chandrika."

"Where is ma'am?" Chandrika whispers.

"She is sleeping. She has had a lot of wine."

"Can you wake her up?"

"She will cry again."

"Listen, Trisha, we have to catch the culprit quickly before he gets away. Any clue will help us find the wretch who committed this crime."

"Let me check, Chandrika."

Chandrika sits on the sofa, her legs trembling with tension. After five minutes, she hears Varunika crying loudly. The sound echoes through the resort making everyone sad. Finally, Trisha opens the door. Chandrika enters quietly and asks Trisha to wait outside. Trisha gives Varunika a reassuring look and leaves the room. Varunika's head is down, luscious hair screening her face.

Chandrika clears her throat and says, "Ma'am…"

Varunika does not reply. After a couple of moments, Chandrika tries again, "Ma'am, if you co-operate we can figure out who the culprit is. We are here to help you. Don't you want the person who murdered your husband to be punished?"

Varunika begins sobbing again, but manages to reply in a muffled voice, "God cannot be so unfair."

She looks at Chandrika, her face wet with tears. Chandrika gives her a tissue to wipe up and says, "Ma'am, please tell me whatever you know." Varunika pulls herself together after wiping her face slowly. It takes some time because many hiccups make their way out forcibly.

"Two months ago, through WhatsApp, I came in contact with a person and we began chatting regularly. At first, things were casual but slowly I started enjoying chatting with him. We shared everything about our lives. In fact, he got to know me so well that sometimes he would tell me what I was wearing on a particular day. Once he even told me what my husband was dressed in. I used to wonder, how can a person tell me such details without even meeting me? I imagined it was someone who lived close by.

I looked around the area and found no one who could fit the bill. Then a thought struck me—perhaps it was one of the other guests at the resort. One day, I had to change into four different dresses for a shoot and my suspicions become stronger when that guy told me exactly which dresses, they were. That's when I was sure he was keeping an eye on everything I was doing. He was a stalker!"

"You never invited him to meet you even once?"

"I did, but he refused to meet. According to him, it was better if we continued to communicate over WhatsApp."

"Do you have his picture?"

"I asked him for one several times and every time he said the same thing, 'I will send you my picture soon'."

Chandrika looks at her diary and rechecks the list of people living at the resort, "So that's why you alleged that one person was the culprit from among the three of them."

Varunika nods.

"Ma'am, a personal question… how was the relationship between Sir and yourself?"

"We had a good relationship."

"Sure?"

Varunika nods again.

"If it was good, then why did you begin an online relationship with a total stranger that you knew nothing about?"

Varunika does not respond. Chandrika adds, "Ishwar said that Hardik used to be out a lot, traveling on work. Is that the reason you felt lonely and got close to the guy on social media?"

This provokes Varunika and she responds furiously, "Look Chandrika, just because I treat you with patience and respect it does not mean you can allege anything."

"Ma'am, I am here to help you. At this moment, we are focused only on finding the culprit. If you suspect someone from the resort, we will conduct a thorough investigation. It should not happen that another angle surfaces later that derails or changes the track of the investigation."

"You may leave now. I will ask SP to send someone else to carry on the investigation."

Chandrika feels insulted. She stands up quickly and moves towards the door.

"Don't leave me alone, I feel trapped," Varunika requests in a small voice. Chandrika immediately melts. She wants to save Varunika at all costs. She gives Varunika a little hug and reassures her that things will be okay.

"He had an affair with another woman while I was at my most vulnerable. We used to fight every day when he was here," Varunika confides tearfully. "I felt insecure and needed someone who cared for me. I liked communicating with the stranger on WhatsApp. He supported me very well emotionally."

"Were Sir's parents aware of what their son was up to?"

"Yes, but they too were as helpless as I was, and couldn't stop him."

"Can I see those chats?"

"Sorry, I have deleted them." Varunika hands over her mobile to Chandrika.

Chandrika looks for any clues but finds nothing, neither in the photo gallery nor in the chat boxes.

"Why did you delete the chat records?"

"I was afraid after hearing the news of my husband."

"Okay, no worries, ma'am, we will recover them."

The mention of chat recovery sends a surge of tension through Varunika. She gets up and lights a cigarette with trembling hands.

Chandrika asks her gently, "Ma'am, is there anything to want to say to me that could possibly be used against you? Now is the time to speak up."

Varunika shrugs, "No, nothing."

"Ma'am, please think it over carefully. Even the slightest of things can turn the investigation in your favor or against it."

"I have already discussed everything with the SP, including an important fact…" Varunika pauses and Chandrika waits eagerly.

"…the guy once asked me on WhatsApp, 'Do you want me to kill your husband?' I thought it was a joke and said, 'Go ahead, kill him'."

Before Chandrika could ask anything further, Varunika adds, "I thought it was just a joke and did not take it seriously. Later, whenever we spoke about Hardik, he reiterated the same thing and I always replied in the same jocular manner. Yesterday, he repeated his question and I foolishly typed, *'Why do you keep asking? Just finish him already'*. I think he took it seriously and killed my beloved." Varunika begins to weep.

"I promise, I will find him ma'am, even if he's deep underground." Chandrika says solemnly.

"I am afraid that if that murderer is not caught, I will be sent to jail."

Chandrika shakes her head. Varunika lights another cigarette and changes track. "I have a plan to make your entry into the world of modeling easy. It's a world where many girls sacrifice everything they have just to get a single chance on the ramp, and even then many don't find success. I can provide you with that chance once all this has been sorted out."

It is clear that Varunika is willing to strike a direct deal with Chandrika. What aunty said was true. Selfishness indeed carried more weight than duty. Chandrika decides to take up Varunika's offer and make them both happy.

❦ ❦ ❦

Chapter - 16

"Do you have a conference room?" Chandrika asks Ishwar. After hearing about his master's death, he's lost. Ishwar does not say anything, but he takes a key from a shelf and motions for Chandrika to follow him to a small conference room near the reception area. Ishwar turns on the lights, removes the covers on the chairs and leaves quietly. Chandrika summons everyone to the meeting room.

'So, my dear friends, you do know why you are here, right?" Girdhari stares at everyone, as a butcher would while choosing which animal to slaughter. The men sit on their respective chairs, fear and apprehension clearly written on their faces. Chandrika glances at a paper and begins the interrogation.

"Ashok, where were you yesterday evening?"

"Ma'am, I just went nearby…" Saransh interrupts.

"Wait… wait for your turn. Do not interrupt and speak only if you are spoken to," Chandrika snaps.

"I was in Chewa village on the Kalka-Shimla route." Ashok stammers.

"At what time?"

"Half-past four."

"What were you doing there exactly?"

"My friend lives there and he owes me money. I had asked him to return it many times, but he just gave me some lame excuses every single time. You know I am without a job and need money to survive. Yesterday, I threatened him with dire consequences if he did not return my money. He agreed to pay up when I spoke to him over the phone. When I got there, however, he was nowhere to be seen. He made a complete fool of me."

"Okay, then what did you do?"

"I called him again and again, but his mobile was switched off."

"Did you not enquire about his whereabouts with his neighbors?" Chandrika continues taking notes.

"He lives in a newly-developed area and the distances between houses are a lot to cover, so I could not ask anyone. Also, I did not want to linger there. The Municipal Department had already forecast bad weather. So, I quickly returned."

"What time did you come back? Was it around 9:00 PM?"

"May be somewhere between 9 to 10 PM. My mobile battery had died by the time I reached so I'm not sure exactly when."

"Can anyone verify your alibi?"

Ashok has no answer.

"Madam just asked you something. Answer her!" Girdhari screamed.

"No ma'am, it was dark in the resort and everybody was in their rooms."

"How did you get here?"

"I took a bus."

"So then, the conductor may recognize you."

Ashok answers without looking at Chandrika, "No, ma'am, I don't think so."

"Well, if you cannot verify your whereabouts, and have no alibi, we have no other choice than to look at you as the prime suspect." Girdhari shocks Ashok with his inference.

"I did not kill anyone!!" Ashok appears more afraid this time but before Girdhari comes near him, he decides it would be better to continue, "I did not purchase a ticket as the bus was overcrowded and the conductor could not reach me. Everyone was in rush to get home quickly."

"Hmm…interesting story." Girdhari directs his sarcasm at Ashok.

❧❧❧

"What about you Ravi?" Chandrika turns.

"I had a client meeting in Mauri village."

"Which is also on the Shimla-Kalka route, is it not?" Chandrika interjects while looking at her notes. "Carry on."

"Just as I arrived there, I realized that the appointment was scheduled for the next day. The weather was gradually turning bad, so I got out my thick raincoat and left for the resort. My bike gave me trouble all the way so it took me a long while to get here. When I finally reached the resort, it was around a quarter to 9:00. I was dead tired and jumped right into bed. After that, I woke up only in the morning when you knocked."

"Okay. So why was your mobile switched off?"

"When I was trying to kick-start my bike, there was a small puddle of water near me and my mobile fell into it. I had to switch it off quickly to prevent electrical damage. Then, this morning I switched it on again."

"Can anyone verify your alibi?"

"As Ashok told you it was dark at the resort."

"But don't you have a bike which creates enough noise to attract anyone's attention."

"Ah, my bike quit on me a kilometer away, so I left it outside a closed shop. I went there around noon when you left the resort, pushed it back, and parked it here."

Chandrika gets Ravi's bike number and color and texts the information to SP Dogra.

⁂

"*Now* it is your turn, my English boy," Girdhari looks at Saransh.

Saransh, however, ignores Girdhari and blurts out, "Ma'am, since the weather in the evening was not a problem for me, I decided to explore the nearby area. I cycled up to the forest. Later, I realized that I was lost and had forgotten the way back." Saransh paused.

Girdhari gives him a sarcastic glance, raises his hands and opens them wide. His face has an expression signifying that he didn't believe a word of what Saransh was saying. Saransh's confidence is shaken for a moment, he turns towards Chandrika to gain some courage.

"What do you mean the weather did not affect you? It was biting cold outside and you went for a joyride?"

"Bro…" Girdhari stares at Saransh who changes his tone, "Sir, I stay in an extremely cold part of Canada and this temperature is quite normal for me."

"What was the time when you came back?" Chandrika asks.

"Ma'am, around 10:00 PM."

"Why does your location show you as being in the resort?"

"I forgot my phone in the room."

"Can anyone support your alibi?"

Saransh thinks for a moment and is unable to reply.

Chandrika completes her notes and arrives at a possible conclusion, "Hardik left this place around 4:00 PM and the rest of you were also not available at that time. I am assuming that the time it takes to travel from this point to wherever the three of you went, is between two to two-and-a-half hours. Your locations have been tracked to the same route that Hardik had taken. Then, for whatever reasons given by you, neither your mobiles are traceable nor do any of you have a verifiable alibi. Am I right?"

"Madam, your analysis is perfect." Girdhari extends his unsolicited support.

"It's highly probable that one of you is the culprit. If you confess to your crime, the punishment will be a bit lenient. If you don't, things are going to get very difficult for you all."

Everyone remains quiet. No one utters a word for fear of being implicated. A few minutes later, Chandrika receives a call. She looks at Girdhari and says, "Dogra sir." She gestures to him that she will take the call outside.

ॐ ॐ ॐ

Girdhari sits down on a chair and acts as if he is busy on his mobile. Saransh feels uneasy and turns to Ravi, "Bro, I have seen you near Varunika's cottage many times. You are a cheap guy and your actions have now got us into trouble… a *lot* of trouble, for no fault of ours. I wish it was you who was murdered, instead of Hardik! I am unnecessarily trapped in this mess." Saransh's voice turns weepy.

"Bullshit! Also, don't call me 'bro'. I am not your brother. Are you not the one always lurking around the resort premises with a camera? And, when someone asks you, what you are up to, all you say is, *I am taking pictures. I love India.*" Ravi imitates Saransh's drawl. "God knows what perverted snaps you take!"

"And you, Ashok…" Ravi now turns to Ashok. "I overheard you one day talking to your friend about a fantasy you had about Varunika. Isn't it true?"

"Shut up, Ravi! That doesn't mean that I am a coldblooded killer. I warn you, do not cross the line!" Ashok raises his hand threateningly.

In response, Ravi punches Ashok who falls off his chair. Ashok retaliates by grabbing Ravi and pushing him towards the wall, while holding him in a lock. Ravi tries to free himself.

Saransh intervenes to stop the fight but Ashok grabs Saransh and says, "You're no saint either."

Ravi uses the opportunity and pushes Ashok so hard that he falls flat on the floor. Through all this, Girdhari continues to be preoccupied with his mobile. He chooses to leave the three guys to sort out the issue amongst themselves. The situation turns uncontrollable. Somehow, Saransh gets punched on the lips and blood oozes out.

Finally, Girdhari has had enough and screams, "Will you bastards keep it down or do you want me to throw all of you in the lock-up?"

Ravi straightens his jacket and Ashok looks at his broken watch.

※ ※ ※

"Girdhariji, please come here." Chandrika peeks inside the room and finds everything is a mess. "What the hell happened here?"

"Everything is fine, madam." Girdhari shoots off an expression which says, *all is fine.*

"Keep an eye on things. If anyone creates too much of a ruckus, shoot them!" Girdhari issues a fake threat and asks a constable to sit inside.

"Yes, sir."

"Girdhariji, I just discussed with Dogra sir and found out that another criminal investigation team is also working on this case. The doctor has completed the autopsy and has shared his report. Let me describe the sequence of events as put together by the investigating team.

Hardik left for Chandigarh in his jeep at around 3:30 PM. It takes two hours to reach there so the murder must have been committed around 5:30 PM. When he neared Kalka, he saw that the checkpost had a long line of vehicles. So, Hardik turned left from the main road onto the unpaved road. After about a half-kilometer, that road rejoins the main road. He must have taken that road to avoid traffic or perhaps to relieve himself.

The culprit had already hidden himself in the back seat of Hardik's jeep. He silently got up from behind him and, before he could figure out what was happening, hit him from behind with an iron rod. The police have found nothing missing from Hardik's body. Neither the expensive wristwatch, nor the wallet full of money and cards was taken. It was a planned murder and was done with one strong blow."

"Hmm…I have a question. How can the police be sure that there was only one person concealed inside the jeep?"

"The back of the jeep was covered only with a transparent thick cover which was clearly captured on different CCTV cameras on the way. The footage shows nobody inside. The culprit must have laid down in the space where passengers keep their legs while seated. And, that space is wide enough to accommodate only one person. After the murder, since there was heavy rain in that area, it has washed away footprints and other evidence. The force of the water was so high that the body was pushed from the narrow road all the way down and it landed on another car. In addition, there are no defensive marks on the body which indicates a lack of a struggle. The water damage makes it very difficult for us to gather DNA evidence too. Also, the murderer was smart enough not to touch any valuable item or he wiped off any possible fingerprints."

"So, when did the murderer hide in the jeep?"

"Two options exist. He may have hidden in the jeep before Hardik left or entered it at one of the checkposts. Hardik once got out of the jeep to buy cigarettes, which was caught on CCTV.

The remaining checkposts confirm that Hardik flashed his VIP status in order to pass though quickly. But for that to happen, he would have had to step out of the jeep again.

Chandrika opens up pictures of Hardik's dead body on her mobile and shows it to Girdhari who looks at them carefully. "Madam, the culprit hit Hardik from behind which means he is…"

Chandrika stops Girdhari, "Yes, our case has almost been solved. Driving back to the resort is a minimum of six hours from where Hardik's body was discovered. The culprit must have returned around 12:00 AM. I also checked yesterday's Google Maps history and it confirmed the timeline. All three of our suspects are missing alibis."

"The culprit must have returned at some time. We can check the number plates of all vehicles returning and find out who he is."

"It is not that easy. For one, a few of the CCTV cameras were not working due to the power cut. Also, from the footage that the team managed to acquire, some of it is useless due to the bad weather conditions that blurred out the video. Even Ravi's bike was captured on the same road but a little later. The team could not identify the bike in subsequent images."

"Hmm… Anyway madam, I am confident that we will catch the culprit."

Chandrika calls out to one of the constables and says, "Go and ask the everyone at the resort some basic questions. Maybe someone saw something." Chandrika also whispers some instructions into the constable's ear and the constable nods.

࿐ ࿐ ࿐

"Listen, guys." Chandrika draws everyone's attention. Chandrika motions to the constable to hand out paper and pens.

"Fill up your details. Name, permanent address, and so on. And sign it at the end. Let's begin with Ashok."

Ashok begins to open the pen's cap but Chandrika stops him. "Not here. Go behind Ravi and Saransh. Sit at the table over there." Ashok stands up and grabs the chair to sit in front of the table. Ravi tries to turn but Girdhari stares him down.

Ashok busies himself with writing while Chandrika and Girdhari observe him carefully. They are sure that Ashok is not the murderer.

"Now you start." Girdhari points to Ravi but he is ignored.

"Hey, you!" Girdhari shouts. Ravi moves along and begins writing at once. Chandrika looks at Girdhari. They are both quite sure that it was Ravi who killed Hardik. But they still need to rule out Saransh. Girdhari does not want to waste any more time. He is eager to return to his son's birthday celebration, "Do you want an invitation to start writing, English boy?"

Saransh immediately leaves his seat, takes the paper, and starts writing. Observing him, both Chandrika and Girdhari are stunned and hold their heads between their palms.

Chandrika stands up and asks Girdhari to come out.

❧ ❧ ❧

"Madam, open up a picture of the dead body." Girdhari is desperate to look at the picture again. Chandrika scrolls through a few images and stops on one of them without wasting a moment. Girdhari gives his baton to Chandrika to hit him from the front. She takes the weapon in her right hand, and pretends to strike Girdhari. The end of the baton comes down on his cheekbone. Now Chandrika holds the weapon with her left hand and stands behind Girdhari.

This time she brings it down slowly to his nape at the back of his head. It ends up just behind the left ear. A mark can clearly be seen in the picture on that very spot, which appears to be the cause of Hardik's death. There is no doubt that the culprit is left-handed.

"Madam, this is a report of everyone," the constable interrupts.

Chandrika and Girdhari glance at each other and mumble, "Trisha, Ishwar and Ramdeen are right-handed, and Shabnam is left-handed."

"What about Kishan?" Chandrika asks.

"Madam, I did not go near him. He was coughing very badly, and Ishwar told me to stay away. I have a family, Madam. I cannot take such risks."

"You can go now. I will check."

❧❧❧

"You're free to leave, Ashok…" Ashok thought he might be hearing things and continued sitting on his chair.

"Hey, did you not listen to what Madam just said?" Girdhari shouts.

"What?" Ashok is still lost in his thoughts.

"You may go now."

"I can go? May I really go, ma'am?" Ashok stammers.

"Now, if you don't go, I will put you behind bars!" Girdhari threatens. Ashok cannot believe his ears. He gets up immediately and exits the room. He also thanks them many times before he exits. Then he enters his room and shuts the door, feeling relieved.

⁂

"Ma'am, why did you let Ashok go?" Ravi musters up the courage to ask.

"Because we don't believe he is the culprit," Girdhari replies curtly.

"What proof do you want, ma'am?"

"Well, your bike was spotted on the road on CCTV, so it means that you went where you say you did, but there is no footage of your returning."

Ravi falls silent. Saransh stammers, "I want to go too…"

"You will be allowed to go my English boy, but first, you need to provide us a valid alibi."

Suddenly, something strikes Ravi and he exclaims, "Wait, wait… I can prove that I have an alibi."

Chandrika approaches him and crosses her arms across her chest.

Ravi continues, "Nearby, about five kilometers away, is an ATM."

Girdhari shrugs, "So what?"

"It was snowing heavily at the time. I entered the ATM and took shelter there for almost half an hour. I am sure the ATM's CCTV has captured me."

"What time was it?" Although Girdhari asks the question to Ravi, he gives Saransh a suspicious look, as if to say, *it looks like Ravi's going to prove himself innocent after all.* Now the ball was in Saransh's hands, just like in the kid's game of Passing the Parcel.

"It was around half-past six."

Chandrika asks for some details and sends them to the cyber cell. They confirm Ravi's alibi right away.

❄ ❄ ❄

Saransh is sobbing and wipes his tears, "Ma'am, I did not do anything. These allegations are totally false."

Chandrika tries to keep him quiet, but he is speaking so loudly that he is unable to listen to anyone. Girdhari, as usual, slaps him and Saransh falls with the chair to the right. Chandrika feels bad for a moment, but she is more focused on catching the culprit and is ready to ignore the law.

"Listen, if your alibi turns out to be valid, I will let you go, I promise. Otherwise, be ready for further interrogation," Chandrika says sternly.

Girdhari grabs Saransh's collar and drags him outside the conference room. Saransh is shouting very loudly, and his voice can be heard far and wide. He keeps repeating the same thing, "I came here around 10:00 PM. I did not kill anyone! Just because I don't have an alibi, it doesn't mean I'm a killer." He's like a poor little lamb crying before heading off to the butcher's cleaver. Girdhari pushes him into a room and locks the door from the outside. He signs to a constable to keep an eye on the room.

Chapter - 17

Day 1 | 7:00 PM

"Sir is happy. He sent a smiley emoji," Chandrika smiles, relaxing. The temperature has dipped even lower and there is vapor coming out of her mouth while speaking. Thank God, the stars can be seen clearly in the sky.

"Can I see it too, madam?" Girdhari requests. He mumbles while reading the message on WhatsApp, "Sir, it gives me great pleasure to inform you that Girdhari and I have got our hands on the culprit. His name is Saransh, and he is an NRI staying at the same resort. He is left-handed and cannot not provide a valid alibi." Some smiley emojis followed.

"Thank you, madam." Girdhari is very happy.

"For what?"

"You mentioned my name."

"Just remember to throw a big party after getting your promotion."

"Yes, madam," Girdhari blushes on hearing these positive words.

"Girdhariji, do we have enough proof to establish that Saransh is the culprit? Is it enough that he doesn't have an alibi?"

"It is very important that he is unable to prove where he was, and don't forget that he is also left-handed. What else do we need? Once we take him into remand, we will be able to prove everything else easily."

"What about the murder weapon?"

"That will also be produced by the police when the time comes."

"How can you be so sure?" Chandrika is highly curious.

"Madam, don't overthink it. We have done our job. Let Dogra sir and the others worry about it now."

Girdhari's mobile starts ringing. He looks at Chandrika and says, "It's my wife's call."

Chandrika nods for him to pick it up.

"Coming darling, I was about to leave. Yes… yes, I will reach in time for the cake cutting," Girdhari assures her.

"You can go, Girdhariji. Our work is mostly done. I will manage," Chandrika says.

"Do you need more constables?"

"Four are enough." Chandrika is confident.

"If you need anything else, call me, madam."

Chandrika gives him a thumbs-up. Girdhari salutes and leaves.

First, Chandrika looks at Varunika's cottage and then at her watch. She wants to inform her parents that she will not be able to make it, or, more precisely, she is no longer interested in meeting the prospective groom. Her goalposts have changed. Chandrika tries to connect with her father but the network is busy.

"Madam, did you drop your key?" someone says from behind her. With her phone to her ear Chandrika turns and sees Kishan. "Yes?"

"Madam, key."

"Where did you find it?" Chandrika notices that the key is in his right hand.

"Near Varunika madam's cottage."

"Thanks!"

"Madam, I saw Saransh sir enter the resort," Kishan adjusts his mask and replies.

"What?" Chandrika is stunned by what she's heard and is unable to react. That one line from Kishan pushes her investigation back to square one.

"Where were *you* yesterday?"

Kishan coughs a couple of times and replies, "In my cabin."

"You were waiting there so that when Saransh came you could confirm his whereabouts?"

"For the past three days, a vehicle has been passing by this road daily, around 10:00 PM. It makes enough noise to disturb my sleep. Yesterday, I was woken up by that noise. After about five minutes, when I looked outside, I saw Saransh sir pushing his bicycle through the snow."

"How did you identify that it was him? The resort's power was out, right?"

"Yes, but there was a lot of lightning as well."

Chandrika did not know what to say, "You can go now. If I need you, I will call you."

Kishan went back to his small cabin. Chandrika calls one of the constables and orders him to find out which big, noisy vehicle passed by the resort every day. Then Chandrika calls Ramdeen to confirm his testimony. Ramdeen had not gone home the previous night. He had decided it would be better to stay at the resort as the weather had turned even worse after 7:00 PM. After their meal, both Ishwar and he had fallen asleep as there was no reason to stay awake. The internet and electricity were out. On top of that, the biting cold had not made things any easier.

Chandrika knocks on the door of Varunika's cottage and Shabnam opens it. Trisha asks Shabnam, "Who is it?"

"Inspector Madam," Shabnam replies.

Chandrika opens the door a little, looks at Trisha and says, "I have a few questions for Shabnam. Where is Varunika Ma'am?"

"She is sleeping upstairs. You may go inside and ask." Trisha starts scrolling through her mobile. "Haven't you already caught the culprit? I heard one of the guys begging to be released."

"Yes, but we are still trying to verify where he was yesterday."

"Meanwhile, you should arrest him."

"The suspect has an alibi but it is not verifiable. We don't have solid proof against him yet." Chandrika does not disclose that they suspected that a left-handed person killed Hardik and that Saransh was left-handed.

Shabnam stands on the porch and Chandrika asks, "Where were you yesterday evening?"

"I was inside all the time due to the bad weather. After I heard a quarrel between Sir and Madam, Madam closed her room on the ground floor and I slept in the adjacent room. I woke up around 12:00 AM. I saw that it was quite dark outside and decided that it's better to stay inside the room."

"What was the quarrel about?"

Shabnam tries to remember and replies slowly, "That I don't know."

"When did you see your Madam after that?"

"In the morning when she was doing her yoga."

"Can you show me your room and Madam's too?"

Shabnam gestures to Chandrika to follow her.

❧❧❧

When Chandrika enters the room, she finds Trisha lying on the sofa with her laptop on her folded legs, "Done?"

"Not yet…"

Trisha shrugs and focuses on her laptop screen again.

❧❧❧

Now Chandrika moves to Shabnam's room. She opens one of the windows a little and tries to look at the adjacent room's window but it is not visible. The parapet is not wide enough to jump outside and the window opens towards the back of the resort.

"Where does your *Sahib* park his jeep?"

Shabnam points in the direction.

Chandrika flashes some light outside the window towards the ground but does not find anything.

Later, Chandrika moves to Varunika's room.

"Did you hear any noise yesterday from this room?"

"What kind of noise are you talking about?"

"Like the sound of someone jumping, or any other kind of noise."

"No."

⁂

Chandrika comes back outside and Trisha asks again, "Done?"

"Yes. But, I have a few questions for you too."

Trisha puts her laptop down and turns serious, "Shoot!"

"When did you see Ma'am and Shabnam after entering the cottage?"

"In the morning."

"And when did you get here?"

"Around 8:00 PM."

"What did you do then?"

"I downed a good quantity of Scotch and knocked on the door which was already open. Then, I fell down while entering… see these scratches on my left hand."

Chandrika raises her own hand to convey, *there is no need to show me your hand.*

"It was difficult to move about. I used my mobile's flashlight and went to my room. When I opened my eyes next, it was morning."

After that, Trisha falls silent.

"Where were you yesterday?"

"What do you mean?" Trisha sounds affronted.

"Trisha, do not take this the wrong way. I need to know your whereabouts." Chandrika tries to be polite and calm.

"So, now, I am on the list of suspects, is it? That is ridiculous! I don't want to say anything."

"Trisha, cooperate with us. If there is anything you can share that might make this murder enquiry easier to solve, I want to know about it. Also, if you do not do so, I am authorized to use another lady constable to convince you."

Trisha's expression says *you don't know my power. Let me teach you a lesson.*

"I was at the Farmhouse."

"Where? With whom?"

Trisha is confident that when Chandrika hears her reply, she will not ask any further questions. "With one of the most influential politicians in the state government. I was there and spent the afternoon with him. Happy?"

Chandrika never expected such an answer and was stunned.

"If you want his name, it's better to call him from my mobile." Trisha unlocks her mobile and enters a number.

"This is just a routine enquiry. Shabnam said that there was a quarrel between Hardik and you two days ago. Is that correct?"

"He was forcing me to sleep with him by flaunting the power of his father," Trisha replies in disgust.

"Was Varunika aware of that?"

"Of course, my dear." Trisha makes her tone very soft and rhythmic.

"Why didn't she say anything?"

"Powerful and popular people have their dark secrets which they don't want revealed, ever!"

Chandrika is still not convinced, and Trisha does not like that. She decides to put pressure on Chandrika for a change.

"Like you, for instance."

"Me?!"

"Yes…you! Today, Varunika spent four to five lakhs on your makeover. Usually, I charge two lakhs from ordinary clients, and for celebrities, around five lakhs or more."

"I did not ask for it!"

"You did not refuse either," Trisha shot back.

"Everyone has their price and the police is no exception. One only needs to find the right amount."

Chandrika feels deeply hurt but she manages to contain her emotions.

"Why don't you ask Varunika if she killed Hardik herself or hired a contract killer?"

"What? What is this bullshit?" Chandrika loses her patience.

"Calm down. It is better if you do as you've been told and not waste my time. Get lost!"

※ ※ ※

Chandrika comes out and is furious. Breathing heavily, she goes into the kitchen where Ishwar is sitting quietly, his eyes red from crying.

"Madam, do… do you want something?" Ishwar asks between sobs.

"Give me some water," Chandrika says abruptly and turns on the television. Every news channel is running the same news. One of the channels is flashing breaking news at the bottom of the screen: *The police has zeroed in on a suspect in the Hardik murder case.*

SP Dogra was to hold a press conference the following morning to reveal the suspect. The press reporter asks multiple questions but the SP refuses to answer. Chandrika knows from SP Dogra's answers who he has inadvertently pointed to. *The news is like a bullet that leaves its gun, never to return.*

Chandrika calls a constable and asks him the findings of a big, noisy vehicle that passed yesterday. The constable says that there are no vehicles on the roads due to the inclement weather.

Chandrika flings her water bottle down in frustration. She sits on a chair holding her head and shaking her legs. She decides it will be better to keep quiet about the latest developments and let the needle of suspicion point to Saransh. She knows, all too well, that it will be difficult to capture the culprit in the short span of time available, given the bad weather conditions.

In some murder cases, it took years to find the culprit. Chandrika is ready to make excuses for her inability to solve the case but is not happy that an innocent person might be sacrificed in the process.

She knows that the circumstantial evidence pointed to a lone suspect. Saransh is left-handed, his location details are missing and his alibi is weak. It's true the security guard, Kishan, had come forward to confirm Saransh's alibi, but he might have seen someone else. At one point, she feels like interrogating Kishan some more but decides it is better to leave it alone.

Instead, she decides to tell Girdhari the next morning, to keep an eye on him to make sure Kishan did not confirm Saransh's testimony. She thinks that once the case is settled, she will approach Varunika with her aspirations.

Chandrika stands up and mumbles, "Okay."

Chapter - 18

Day 2 | 6:00 AM

It is early morning and the sun is yet to rise. The police force has placed barricades at the main gate to prevent the media and other spectators from entering the resort. Jeeps with red and blue lights and loud sirens crisscross the area. Ishwar serves Chandrika a glass of tea.

Although the small hot glass feels like a blessing from God in the freezing cold climate, Chandrika does not enjoy it much. Her legs shake restlessly, sometimes up and down and sometimes from side to side.

The sun rose and the snowy peaks reflected its golden light bringing a certain calmness to the mind. Chandrika looks at the serene sight and stops quivering. The policemen check their wireless radios and confirm the arrival of the team.

Varunika's parents and her sister have arrived there around 5:00 AM and their cries could be heard outside the cottage.

Finally, a huge convoy of white cars arrives and a policeman moves the barricades for it to pass. The crowd outside has by now swelled and includes national TV channels, fans and supporters of Varunika. Correspondents are busy with their mics and begin covering the news in their own ways.

SP Dogra, Inspector Negi, and the IGP (Inspector General of Police) of Haryana, Hooda, step out from their white vehicles. One of the bodyguards helps Mr. Dawan out of his vehicle. He assists him to the cottage. Ishwar has already arranged chairs around a big table under a covered shed in the parking lot. One of the policemen brings Saransh, while a lady constable goes to bring Varunika. She is dressed in white, has sunglasses on, and comes out with her family. Mr. Dawan remains inside.

⁂

Everyone sits down together. The technical team too is allocated some space to setup their desks and work on the evidence.

"You may proceed," Hooda says in his deep voice.

Dogra clears his throat and replies, "Sir, the case is very clear. This person, an NRI, came to India a while ago and checked into this resort. Over time, he developed affections for Varunika, which were one-sided. Then, when he did not receive a favorable response, he became frustrated. To escape detection, he went out and bought a burner SIM card and began using it to communicate with her without revealing his identity."

On hearing Dogra's narrative, everyone turns to look at Saransh whose eyes are cast down with shame. Dogra stops and Hooda says, "Proceed. I am listening."

"Okay, sir. This person, whose name is Saransh, got more and more desperate as time went by and finally crafted a plan to kill Hardik. He thought that was the only way he could get Varunika's attention. Saransh got the opportunity he was waiting for two days ago. When he found that Hardik was to leave from the resort, he hid in Hardik's jeep, and at the opportune moment, struck him from behind on the head with a heavy iron rod."

"Have you found the murder weapon?"

"Not yet. That's why we need to remand the suspect for two weeks."

"We will not remand him to you because this murder has occurred in Haryana. What sort of other evidence have you collected?"

"We have found Varunika's pictures on his camera."

Chandrika hands over the pen drive to the technical team, and they begin examining it.

"No, no, no! This is not solid proof. Sometimes fans of celebrities go crazy and end up taking pictures of them. That is not a crime."

Dogra looks at Saransh and explains, "Sir, we have reason to believe that Hardik was murdered by a left-handed person and Saransh here, is left-handed."

"Show me the list of all the people staying at this resort."

Chandrika presents the list. On it there are two other people who are also listed as left-handed. Hooda glances through it quickly.

"Call the others too. I want to see them."

The constable calls Ravi. "What about him? Have you verified his alibi?" Hooda looks at Chandrika.

"Yes, sir. When our technical team analyzed the location data, they found out that Ravi was sheltering in an ATM at the time of the murder."

"What about this Sheela… no, Shabnam?" Hooda corrects himself.

Shabnam is waiting by the lady constable. "She is incapable of carrying out anything like this."

Hooda has no doubt about Shabnam after seeing her personality. He is sure that she could not harm an insect, let alone a person.

Hooda turns his gaze to Dogra, "As per your report and my understanding, you do not have sufficient evidence besides the fact that Saransh does not have an alibi. And remember that around 10 percent of people in the world are left-handed. So, this could just be a coincidence."

"Sir, but what about the phone number from which he used to harass Varunika?"

Varunika unlocks her phone, and Dogra hands it over to the technical team. Hooda glances through the evidence but finds nothing in the chat records. Dogra quickly presents a hard copy of the recovered chats to Hooda before he can get annoyed.

"Look at this chat for instance. It is clear that the accused used to trouble Varunika."

"Most of the chat looks harmless, except for the parts where he talks about killing Hardik and Varunika urges him to kill her husband." Hooda sounds a little confused and Dogra pounces on the opportunity. Although Varunika was the one who told Dogra about the WhatsApp chats after Hardik's murder, he uses the information smartly to garner Hooda's confidence.

"Sir, it was under my orders that we kept a vigil on the accused. Let me explain to you. The SIM card was purchased using a fake identity. Even though the phone was kept under surveillance, this guy turned out to be highly crafty and we could never clearly track his location."

"Did you inform Hardik about the threat to his life?"

"Yes, sir," Dogra lies confidently.

"So why was he left alone yesterday?"

"Apparently, he told the constable not to come."

Hooda looks at one of the constables and raises his eyebrows. "And the constable accepted?" The constable remains quiet and expressionless, "We will conduct an enquiry into that for sure."

Hooda is unable to comprehend what to do next. He feels like something is amiss but can't put his finger on it. He returns the papers to the team.

"So what do you want now?" Hooda is perplexed.

"We would like the suspect to be remanded to us for two weeks."

"Alright," Hooda gives his permission, reluctantly.

Dogra's wish is finally fulfilled but he hides his happiness.

Chapter - 19

Day 2 | 9:00 AM

The sun is gradually turning bright, the show is done, and Saransh sits quietly waiting for the formalities. God, though, had a different fate in store for him. The mysterious phone gets activated and one of the vigilance team members reports, "Sir, the SIM just became active."

"Find its location, quickly!" Hooda is excited. Varunika's phone was already in Hooda's hand and a WhatsApp message appears on it with a beep: *Ma'am, I am your biggest fan and as per your instructions to kill your husband, I have done it! Our task has been accomplished.*

A couple of teams move out in the direction of the phone's last location along with sniffer dogs. Media teams follow them at close quarters. Within ten minutes, the police surround a hut and recover the phone but don't find anybody present.

"The accused must have seen us and appears to have absconded," Hooda says to Dogra. The sniffer dogs are given the phone to smell, and the police teams begin following them. The squads, however, find that the dogs appear confused and begin retracing their steps after a certain point on the track. Finally, they just end up going round in circles. All their efforts have been vain.

"Let's go back to the resort," Hooda orders.

⁂

"I think there is something fishy going on here, Dogra. This matter appears to be different from the picture you painted."

"Maybe, sir." Dogra looks downcast

"So now, we must arrest Varunika on conspiracy charges and question her."

Chandrika looks at Varunika who turns pale on hearing this. Trisha is by her side to reassure her.

"What are you saying, sir? You think that Varunika has killed her own husband? How is that possible?" Dogra did not expect such a turn of events and comes forward to save Varunika.

"Dogra, look at it logically. Saransh is in front of me, so he couldn't have sent the message we just received. Right? So it is obvious that someone else is involved and has confessed to killing Hardik. Don't you think this could be a case of contract killing?"

"So we should arrest that person who is the real killer," Dogra looks frustrated.

"You do that and present him in front of me. And if Varunika is not guilty, I will release her."

"I understand your point, sir. Shall I conduct her interrogation at our station?" Dogra requests.

"No, Dogra. It's too late for that. Now, she will be taken to Haryana where she will be on remand for two weeks. One thing you must remember is that until you find the murderer, Varunika will be considered the prime suspect."

"Sir…"

"No, I am not going to listen to anything." Hooda asks the lady constable to take Varunika into custody and also to allow the press conference to happen inside.

Varunika begins to cry and looks at her parents for support, but they are helpless. Correspondents try to catch Varunika's grim mood in their cameras, but Hooda stops them. All cameras and mics then turn to Hooda and Dogra because all of a sudden, everyone has a lot of unanswered questions.

Saransh is released, but he is still scared.

❉ ❉ ❉

Around 11:00 AM, the resort falls silent. Everyone has left. Trisha is packing her bags, when Chandrika knocks on the door.

"Come in!!" Trisha shouts. For a few seconds, nothing is said. Trisha wants to say, *hey you are useless and could not save Varunika.*

Chandrika stands firmly and says, "Here are your dresses. I want to return them to you along with the other accessories. I don't want all this anymore."

Trisha is not expecting this. Chandrika continues, "Also, the next time you threaten me by throwing a VIP's name, mark my words, I will not spare you or them as well. Watch how you speak to a police officer!"

Trisha does not respond, and avoids eye contact with Chandrika.

"One more thing, I will pay you whatever you charge, two lakhs or more, in EMIs. WhatsApp your details and I will take care of it." Chandrika throws Trisha a disgusted look and leaves the room.

Saransh, Ravi and Ashok pack their bags and prepare to leave the resort. They have had enough of their ordeal. Saransh gives Chandrika a look that says, *because of you my life was almost thrown into deep shit.* Chandrika avoids looking at him.

❧ ❧ ❧

Day 1 | 7:30 PM

Chandrika's Story

I was angry and came back to the conference room to play a round of darts to calm myself down. None of them hit their target. My shots were not as precise as they should have been. I wanted to slap Trisha hard, but my false ambition was so overpowering that it did not allow me to. My setup had been spoilt by Kishan. Just a half hour ago, I was happy and suddenly it had all been snatched away. I thought Dogra sir would handle the situation, but he just wanted the high-profile case to turn in his favor.

My thoughts continued to pester me, until I began to ask myself the question, *if Saransh is not the culprit, who can it be?* It was imperative to find the real culprit before dawn, otherwise it would be too late and he would get away forever.

I entered Varunika's name in the Google search bar. The internet was working intermittently. I went through various results, news clips, award ceremonies, her journey through life, marriage and many other things. However, nothing really stood out. I felt even more frustrated and began flinging darts at the board again with the same sad results.

For a moment, a spark lit up in my mind and I entered 'Hardik Dhawan' into the search engine. This time I found a lot of people connected to him. After scrolling and checking their profiles and news about them, I stopped at one particular news clip,

The court had declared Hardik innocent in an earlier murder case and another person, Aadarsh, had been convicted and sentenced to life imprisonment. I found that interesting and thought it would be better to go the Police Headquarters in Shimla to find out more. I called Ramdeen and asked him to take me there.

༚ ༚ ༚

Day 1 | 8:15 PM

I started the computer and accessed some old cases. Finally, I found the case files of the 15-year-old murder. As I skimmed through the information, I was conscious that time was flying by. I wanted to slow it down but unfortunately, we humans do not have that power. I was surprised when I saw an old picture of Varunika among the other witnesses, and also found her statement. It was against Aadarsh, the main accused. He had been awarded life imprisonment for the murder of an Anglo-Indian man, Mr. John D'Costa, in Shimla. I looked up pictures of the main accused, Aadarsh, clicked in jail during different events.

In one, he was eating some rice and I noticed that he held the spoon in his right hand. In another picture, he was holding a trophy, this time too with his right hand. My search had hit a dead end again. I asked myself, *can a right-handed person hit another from behind with a heavy weapon using his non-dominant hand, with so much force to cause death?*

I decided to conduct a test. I found a heavy iron rod, much like the murder weapon, picked it up with my left hand, and tried to hit something but just could not generate enough force to do much damage.

During the course of Aadarsh's imprisonment, he had requested parole twice. One when his mother passed away within nine months of him being in jail, and the second time, four years into the sentence, at the time of his father's death. He was granted parole only on the second occasion for five days. I read more deeply about the case and the sentence and realized that Aadarsh was 20 years old when this incident happened.

An excerpt from the judgement: *At an age when young people set out to make something of their lives, Aadarsh was possessed by the greed for money which led him on a path of crime.*

The victim, Mr. John D'Costa was a reputed man in his community and his father had received many medals during World War II for his service to the country. I reject the death penalty for the accused as it is not the rarest of the rare cases, but the accused has been found guilty of murder in the first degree, and thereby I sentence him to life imprisonment.

I glanced at the evidence list and it listed an employee ID-card, a broken flower pot and a pillow. I went to the storeroom and opened an almirah where the evidence was supposed to be stored in a plastic bag. All the three items were in there as described in the list. However, there was also a cigarette butt in a very peculiar color. It was a foreign brand, the same one Varunika smoked. That butt had not been presented in court. At that moment, I was not sure whether Aadarsh killed Hardik or not.

Day 1 | 9:00 PM

The Flashback

I ordered Ramdeen to take me back to the resort. Nobody was on the roads except for a few tourists in their four wheelers, passing by. All the shops were closed. I found a liquor shop that was open and stepped in to purchase half a bottle of brandy. The news channels were running Dogra sir's statement repeatedly. He had given a statement about half an hour ago to the media speaking about how we were on the verge of a major breakthrough, *where a young boy is involved.* I mumbled in frustration, *shit.* The shopkeeper eyed me suspiciously which I did not like, so I showed him my ID-card.

"Sorry, ma'am," he mumbled. Although I had seen a good variety of liquor in Varunika's cottage, I was in no mood to bother Trisha; she had already insulted me enough.

I closed my eyes and began eliminating people who were staying at the resort one by one. Finally, I realized that I knew a lot more about everyone except Kishan. His alibi hadn't been checked by anyone. Where was he that evening, exactly? My intuition told me that Aadarsh and Kishan were related somehow. I started to rewind everything that I had observed about Kishan. Like when he handed over my key, when he used a spade to remove snow near the gate, and even earlier, when he threw the ball. That's when I remembered that he had stopped the ball and hit it back with the palm of his left hand. That hit was important to me. I was confident… *Aadarsh is Kishan*, I decided to catch him red-handed.

※ ※ ※

Kishan lit a fire with some wooden logs for the constables to keep warm. He built a fire for himself as well, but away from the others, behind a thick tree. The cold grew worse as the night deepened. I sat in front of Kishan who was rubbing his palms over the fire to warm himself. My watch showed 9:30 PM.

"I am waiting for the truck you told me about earlier which passes through here at 10:00 PM," I said politely.

Kishan did not reply. His impassive face and stone-cold eyes did not reveal what was going on in his mind. I slowly sipped some brandy knowing that my tolerance for alcohol was good. I tried to call my father to inform him that I would not be coming to Chandigarh but my phone just refused to connect to the network. At five minutes to ten I looked at Kishan. He was clearly avoiding my gaze and rubbing his palms softly. Suddenly, my phone rang. It was my father.

"Where are you? We are worried about you. Is everything all right?"

"I am good, Papa, but I am stuck here on this case. You have seen the breaking news from Shimla that has been flashing on all channels, haven't you?" I replied calmly.

"You mean the one involving Varunika's husband?"

"Yes, Papa."

"So you are not coming, is it?" Papa sounded upset.

"How can I come, Papa?" I emphasized each word to show the importance of the matter.

"Tomorrow Daksha is leaving… and he will be abroad for a whole year." Papa sounded distraught.

"Papa, I am not interested in marriage. Have you seen the new picture I sent you?" I asked hopefully. Papa ignored me.

"For the first time I feel like I am talking to an immature girl. You told me…"

I heard the loud creak of an old lorry. I immediately put my phone down and ran towards the constables who were soaking up the heat from the fire.

"There it is! Stop that lorry!" I glanced at my watch; it was exactly a quarter past ten. One of the constables ran towards the gate, he slipped on some muck on the slope and sprained his left foot. The second constable went after him to help him up. The third ran after the truck but his foot got miserably stuck in the red, muddy soil.

"Sorry, madam, it is difficult to run on this slushy ground. If you like, I can follow the truck on my bike," the constable said.

"It's okay. How is Jubair?"

Jubair was wincing in pain. I asked one of the other constables to get a pain reliever from Ishwar.

Chapter - 20

I went a little away to call Dogra sir.

"Hello, Chandrika. What's the matter?" Dogra sir picked up my call quickly.

"Sir, I have some doubts about Saransh. I think there is a slight chance that he is not the culprit as we suspect. I need more time to further investigate some leads and try to find the real culprit."

"Earlier, you said that you were sure that Saransh is the culprit. I have given an official statement and cannot retract it until and unless you get solid proof that someone else is the perpetrator. We were already on a tight deadline with the media at our heels and now you are requesting for more time."

I did not know what to say. Dogra sir was right about the time constraint.

"Listen Chandrika, let's just stick to our story. Is that clear?"

"Yes, sir," I replied meekly.

I sipped some more brandy. A few blocks of wood were slightly wet and were crackling in the fire. I took out my diary and started to take notes.

"Tell me your details, your name, address, mobile number... everything."

Kishan was about to start when I stopped him for a moment. Alcohol had impaired my ability to perform even the simplest of tasks such as sharpening my pencil. Kishan offered to help. I gave him the sharpener and the pencil. He did it quickly and returned them.

Writing too was difficult under the influence of the brandy and I ended up breaking the point again. "Sor... ry..." I slurred. Kishan raised his hand to reach for the sharpener but this time I watched carefully and saw that he held the sharpener with his left hand. He, however, was unable to sharpen the pencil easily. That was enough for me to realize that I had indeed caught him red-handed.

I took out the service revolver issued to me at the Police Headquarters, "Enough of your games. You can fool us no longer." Kishan had held the sharpener in his left hand. I added, "You are ambidextrous, you use both hands, and such people make up only one percent of the population. Also, it is usually left-handed people who develop this capability. You made a perfect plan to hide your identity but this tiny sharpener has made you reveal your dirty little secret. This sharpener is made only for left-handed people."

Kishan was not ready to except my explanation. The time it took him to shave the pencil with his left hand was the same as it was with his right.

"You are over smart. Use this one, the one I gave you the first time."

Kishan looked at it as if to say, *what is the difference?* First, he tried to sharpen it with his right hand and it took longer than expected.

I then gestured with my head for him to do it with his left hand and he did it faster than before.

"Got it…" I retorted. "This sharpener is made specially for left-handed people. The first time I gave you a rusty one which you have now. I thought you must have tried and could not sharpen the pencil with your right hand as it requires a lot of force.

The psychology of the accused is usually to work fast so no one pays much attention to them. And more often than not, that is the point when they make mistakes. What you failed to realize was that it was a trick set to expose you."

Kishan sat dumbfounded and continued to stare at the logs in the fire.

"You are Aadarsh not Kishan who has completed 14 years in jail! I went through your case history from the files at the Police Headquarters. I did not have enough time to go through them all, but I will. I can also call a handwriting expert to verify your old signatures and prove my case. However, it will be better for you if you tell me yourself."

"You cannot change your statement," he said. "You have already sent the information to your seniors and it is all over the news."

"Kishan, I just want to hear the truth." I lowered my voice not wanting to alert my team's attention.

"You cannot go back on your statement now, they are not interested in digging out old graves," he persisted.

"Listen, if you don't cooperate, I will shoot you." Although I threatened him, he showed no sign of concern.

"I'm not afraid of you," he said disdainfully, "but due to the police department's VIP-oriented mentality, an innocent person is trapped in a web of lies."

I placed my revolver back in my holster and looked at Kishan, waiting for him to speak.

After a pause, he continued, "A story was famous in our jail. During the British era, one jailer was well-known for his atrocities against the inmates. His had one stone eye, and it was difficult to identify which one was natural and which was artificial. Whenever he inspected a jail, he would line up all the inmates and say, "The person who identifies which one of my eyes is fake will be released immediately."

No one dared to give it a shot since they were all positive that the one who got it wrong would be in for some kind of unpleasant surprise in the future. Then one day, one of the inmates came forward and dared to identify the fake eye. And, by a stroke of luck, got it right. He was released immediately. Before releasing him, the jailer asked, "How did you volunteer to guess something that no one had the courage to do before?"

The inmate replied, "Your fake eye looks less ferocious compared to your natural one."

"I can't make out anything of that sort from your eyes. They both appear identical and emotionless," I said, knowing it was not related to our situation.

In response, Kishan took a second and then removed the contact lens from his right eye. An expression of revenge was clearly visible in it.

"Madam, when you came in this morning your eyes were innocent and honest, but gradually they filled up with anger, ambition and dishonesty," he said.

For the first time I felt guilty.

҂ ҂ ҂

Aadarsh's Story

"I was the only son of my parents. When I was 19 years old, I worked in a courier company. Varunika, I mean Garima, worked in a private bank. Anyone who caught a glimpse of her could not help but admire her beauty and mannerisms. I had a huge crush on her. I knew that I was not her only admirer. Many men would jump at a chance to visit her bank just to look at her pretty face, a face so mesmerizing that it did not allow me to sleep at night sometimes.

She always smelled like a flower garden and men buzzed around her like bees. She was an ideal girl, pretty, demure and well-mannered. I knew I was no match for her beauty, but my desires only got stronger each time I looked at her. One day, she accidentally touched me while handing over a checkbook for delivery. It sent a shockwave through my system. I realized how strong and deep my love for her had become.

I knew most of the customers who held accounts in the bank because it was I who usually couriered deliveries from the bank to them. Mr. John D'Costa was one such customer. He was an old man who lived alone as his son had settled in Australia. I often visited his house and he used to open a small window built into his door to collect his parcel.

Meanwhile, Garima had begun dating Hardik. I had noticed them together in many restaurants and sometimes when he dropped her off at the bank. I once heard someone from the bank inquiring about their relationship and she shrugged it off saying *they were just casual friends.*

Then one day, I noticed that Garima, was upset. In fact, she had been so for a whole week. I mustered up the courage and asked, 'What happened ma'am? You look very upset.'

Garima replied in her sweet voice, 'It's nothing. Everything is fine.'

I again asked, 'Ma'am, I can see that you are hiding something. You may be able to control your facial expressions but not the feelings being reflected in your beautiful eyes. They say everything.'

For a minute, Garima did not respond. She then offered to share a cup of coffee with me at a nearby restaurant. I felt happy and proud, and accepted her offer gladly. She ordered two cups of coffee.

❃❃❃

'Do you know, my ambition is to become a successful model? I belong to a middle-class family and my father cannot afford the money required to launch a career in the glamour industry,' she confided.

'Ma'am, so what would you really like to do?' I sipped my coffee.

Garima looked into my eyes, 'I want to go to Mumbai and try my luck.'

'Yes, ma'am, you certainly must go. With your looks, you will be unstoppable.' I got a little excited at the idea.

Garima placed her coffee mug on the table and said, 'That is easier said than done. I need money… a lot of money.'

'How much?'

'Around seven lakhs to be really comfortable, but I can manage with even five lakhs.' Garima looked at me hopefully.

I desperately wanted to help her but that amount of money was out of my reach. Then suddenly something clicked in my mind. My father had sold an old shop of ours near the railway station and had received four lakhs from the sale. He had kept it safely in the almirah.

I offered, 'Ma'am, I can arrange four lakhs for you.'

'Oh really?! I suppose I can manage on four lakhs too.' Garima appeared charged up all of a sudden.

She gently placed her palm on mine, sending another shockwave through my body. 'When can you get me the money? By tomorrow morning?'

'Yes, I can.'

'And don't worry. I will return the amount to you as soon as I get my first big break. You know how much money models are paid, right?'

I was confident that Garima would definitely get her break and rise to the top of the fashion industry. I gave her the four lakhs wrapped in an old newspaper. She took one month to leave and caught a flight to Mumbai. I saw Garima and Hardik at the airport and would have avoided them, but Garima called me over and introduced us. She then gave me a little hug and waved goodbye.

❦ ❦ ❦

After she left for Mumbai, I did not feel like going to the bank anymore. I felt lonely and bored in Shimla. After a long time, I walked into the bank just to get a look at Garima's desk which had been vacant for the last three weeks. To my astonishment, Garima was sitting at her desk. I went straight to her and asked, 'Ma'am, you are back! What happened?'

Garima looked visibly upset and forced a smile to her face, 'Can we meet this evening at the same place we did last time for coffee?'

'Yes, ma'am!' I felt a wave of happiness flow through me. Shimla appeared beautiful once again.

⁂

Garima and Hardik arrived at the restaurant 30 minutes after I did. I followed her nod and joined them. Hardik shook my hand. A waiter served us three coffees. Garima quickly glanced around the restaurant to make sure that nobody was within hearing range.

She then said in a low voice, 'Aadarsh, I have to pay you back your four lakhs.' I did not react. Money was not the question for me. Four lakhs was a small amount to pay to make the one I loved happy, and I was ready to offer her more. Unfortunately, I only had that amount, which I had stolen from my home and given her. My poor father was still not aware of my evil deed.

'I have already spent most of what you have given me in Mumbai but was not able to accomplish what I had set out for. I need more money, Aadarsh,' Garima pleaded.

I wanted to say, *yes, yes, I will help,* but my expression said, *how*??

'Aadarsh, I have a plan for that. Do you know John D'Costa?'

'*Buddha Baba* (the Old Man)?'

'Yes. I know that he withdrew ten lakhs from the bank today to purchase a new property. He plans to pay it to the seller in question when his son visits India next week.'

'What's that got to do with us?' I was perplexed.

Garima and Hardik exchanged glances. She gestured for me to come closer, 'We have to steal that money from D'Costa. I will take that money and head off to Mumbai again. I am positive I will make it this time and you will get your four lakhs back too.'

'Oh no, ma'am! That is a crime. Why can't Hardik help you with the money instead? I know he comes from an affluent family.' I gave Hardik a look of disgust that he obviously did not like.

He controlled himself and replied, 'You're right, this is not a big amount for me. But just last month my father paid out 20 lakhs as payment when I lost a cricket bet. My father is very annoyed at me for that, and I cannot ask him for money right now.'

I had heard enough so I stood up, took my bag, and left the place. Garima called out to me from behind, 'Listen, Aadarsh…'

I did not stop."

Chapter – 21

"I was upset when I reached home. My father looked sad and the almirah was open. He was crying and held my shoulder, '*Beta*, my four lakhs have gone missing. Have you seen it?'

'No… no, Papa,' I stammered.

'Come… I want you to come with me to lodge a police complaint.'

'Wait… Papa.' On hearing him mention the police, I blurted out the truth, 'I took the money and gave it to a friend who needed it urgently.'

My father was shocked, 'Are you a fool? Do you know why I sold my one and only property? It was for your mother. She is a heart patient and needs open heart surgery. I had arranged for that money to pay for the operation and medical expenses. The operation has been scheduled next month.'

I was dumbstruck and did not know what to say or do. I felt guilty that I had inadvertently pushed my mother into the jaws of death.

҈ ҈ ҈

'What is your plan?' I asked Garima the next day. We met at the same restaurant as the day before.

Garima glanced at Hardik, turned to me, and explained, 'Tomorrow afternoon, when most people will be indoors, you will go for the courier delivery. When D'Costa opens the little window on his door to receive his package, you must make your move. Your face will be covered with a cap lowered to your forehead. Be careful when you show your identity card. Hold it in such a way that your thumb remains partially over the picture and name.' I nodded in confirmation.

'Perfect! Garima and I will be at the door to the left and right respectively. Our faces will be obscured by handkerchiefs and our heads covered with caps.

D'Costa will not open his door unless you start coughing desperately and ask him for water. We'll enter behind him once he opens the door. Then we'll seize and hold him. The money must be around somewhere. It only has to be found. You wait outside and warn us if anyone approaches.'

Garima read my face and figured out that I did not like the plan, 'Don't worry about Mr. D'Costa. Once I get modeling assignments, I will return all his money with interest,' she reassured me putting her hand on mine. This time, however, I did not feel anything.

'Okay.' Although the plan looked simple and I could trust Garima, my heart was palpitating with an unknown fear.

༠༺ ༠༺ ༠༺

As per the plan, I picked up Hardik and Garima. All the three of us rode on the same bike and reached John D'Costa's cottage. I parked the bike outside the compound, opened the iron gate as quietly as possible, and rang the doorbell, my heart beating rapidly.

Ding dong!

I pulled my cap as low over my forehead as possible, so no one would recognize me. After five minutes, the unfortunate old man opened the tiny window on the door. I showed him my ID-card and quickly took it back. I kept my voice very low, "Courier, sir."

The old man received his letter and signed my record sheet. Then he turned to go inside. As soon as he did that, I immediately began coughing like I was going to throw up my insides. When he looked back at me, I signed for some water. At first, he ignored me, but I continued to cough and choke. Finally, he opened the door. In the meantime, Garima and Hardik had already covered their faces, donned their gloves, and were ready for the next step. As soon as the door was slightly open, they pushed it open completely and entered. From outside, I could see clearly what was going on inside the living room.

My next task was to wipe away any fingerprints on the doorbell and any other possible surfaces that I might have touched. Hardik closed the door and Garima started searching for the key. A key chain was displayed on a wall. Garima seized the key ring and began experimenting with the keys on the cabinet. D'Costa was struggling but he was not strong enough to break free from Hardik's powerful grip. Hardik had put his palm around D'Costa's mouth and held him down on the sofa in an iron grip. I was just a lowly spectator.

Finally, Garima found the bag of money which contained the ten lakh rupees. Suddenly, D'Costa, in desperation, bit Hardik's hand which caused him to loosen his grip. D'Costa took that opportunity and ran towards the door. Garima tried to stop him by grabbing his shirt, but he fought back and, during the scuffle, the old man wrenched Garima's mask off! He recognized her instantly and was shocked.

On seeing D'Costa's stunned expression, Garima felt she was looking at her guilty face in a mirror. Hardik got up, grabbed the old man, and threw him on a nearby bed. Then he covered his face with a pillow. D'Costa fought for breath. In the ensuing struggle, his hand hit a nearby flowerpot which fell to the ground.

Garima grabbed his hands to control him further. It worked. D'Costa stopped struggling. After a few minutes his body stopped moving altogether. I knew something had gone horribly wrong and I had done nothing to prevent it. When they finally pulled off the cushion from his face, what they saw sucked the breath out of them. The old man was lying on the bed, motionless, his eyes wide open. I knew nothing more could be done so I ran towards the gate. There, I got on the bike and turned it on, ready to make our getaway.

Garima came out of the house smoking a cigarette, the butt of which she threw near the gate. It was as though she had accomplished a great task. Both, Hardik and Garima had removed their masks and gloves so that they would not look suspicious. I revved the bike after we had all piled on, and zoomed off. We had only crossed a hundred meters when I lost control of the bike due to the uneven path and hit one of the other residents who was walking there. He was flung to one side, and we all fell to the other.

I suppose the resident, Mr. Matthew, was going to meet Mr. D'Costa. We, however, got up, jumped onto the bike and sped away for fear of being spotted. We did not stop to see what had happened to Mr. Matthew. He was groaning in pain and cursing us."

☙ ☙ ☙

Chapter – 22

"'What did you do ma'am?' I asked Garima. My voice was full of worry. We had reached the same location from where we had started. By then it was noon. No one was around except us.

'We had no other option…' Hardik started saying.

I shouted, 'Will you please shut up!'

'Calm down, Aadarsh, nothing will happen.' Garima gave me a glass of water.

I took one look at the black bag full of crisp new notes and pounced. I wanted my share of the money right away. Garima held my hand, 'Hey, don't be stupid. These are all new notes and if you spend them anywhere, you will be caught immediately.' I felt vulnerable and stopped myself. I felt like, *a thirsty person, who had found a glass of pure, cool water in front of him but couldn't even have a sip.*

'Hardik plans on exchanging the currency for old bills so that the numbers will not be in sequence.' Garima looked Hardik and he nodded.

'How long will it will take?' I was desperate.

'More than a month,' Hardik replied immediately.

I held my head tightly for a minute and said reluctantly, 'Okay… what about that old man whom we hit on the way?'

'I don't think he noticed us. He was wearing spectacles with thick lenses and when you hit him, those fell off. In any case your face was mostly covered up with a cap. Don't worry.'

For a second, I calmed down but in the very next second, alarm bells rang in my head. 'Where is my ID-card?'

Everybody panicked, 'Look in your pocket.' I ran my hands through all my pockets but the miserable ID-card was nowhere to be found. I racked my brain for a few moments and scary possibilities came up. When we fell from the bike after hitting Matthew, it must have either fallen on the road, or worse, it had fallen on Matthew and he had got hold of it. If that turned out to be the case, the police would be on us soon.

'Oh, God' Garima groaned.

'Ma'am, if the police finds me, I will have to tell them everything!' I was panicking big time.

Hardik interrupted, 'You will do no such thing. Just do as I say. Got it? Follow my instructions and everything will be okay.'

'Why should I obey you and follow your rules?'

'You have to, my dear. What other choice do you have?'

'I did not murder anyone. Why should I be afraid? The charges laid on me will be nothing compared to what you two will face. Also, I am the eye-witness in this case and can strike a deal with them.'

Garima was quiet and looked blank like her mind had stopped working. Hardik said, 'What is important to you? Your life, money, or a stupid confession that will get you nothing? If you tell the truth, the only thing certain is you will not get your four lakhs back and then your innocent mother will have to face dire consequences. Think about that.'

I drank a glass of water and tried to cool down, 'Fine! Tell me what to do next.'

'The police might try to get in touch with you. Stay calm and cooperate, or surrender if required. When they ask you about the murder, just deny any involvement. Say you went there to steal the money because you needed it for your ailing mother's operation. Then tell them that when you reached D'Costa's house, the door was open, and he was already dead. You searched for the money but did not find it. Then, thinking that the murderer might have found the money and taken it, you panicked and left. On the way, we asked you for a lift. Since Garima and you know each other, you agreed. Then, on the way, you lost control of the bike and it hit Matthew. Clear?'

I revised the story a couple of times while Hardik kept adding, 'The judge will consider that your intention in entering the house was only for robbery. Also, we did not leave any other traces behind that can be used as evidence against us.

Another thing, never hire a lawyer for yourself. Ask for one from the government instead. That will show that you are poor and cannot afford a lawyer of your own. Also, don't worry. We have already done this sort of thing a couple of times earlier. Garima informs me about the soft targets and I do my groundwork perfectly. Our teamwork is so good that no one has been able to get to us till now.' That came as a shock to me. I could not believe that the person that I loved, was a heartless criminal. I gave her a disgusted look, but could do no worse as I was helpless.

As expected, the police traced me and I was arrested. I did as I was told. My lawyer was wise enough to construct a case in such a way that no charges of theft were brought against me. Also the police did not find any money on me no matter how much they searched. But I was unable to escape the murder allegation. The Trial Court sentenced me to 14 years in prison. My lawyer informed me, 'Don't worry, *the dispute will be addressed in the High Court. Your money has already been handed to your father.'*

I remained silent as I waited for my case to be heard in the High Court. I waited a long time and received no response. After that, I had to face the worst. I was often beaten and harassed in jail. Each day I passed behind bars, it became more and more difficult for me to survive. I was happy however that my father had got back his money. I assumed that my mother would be better now.

While I was inside, I got news of my mother's passing. My father requested that I be given parole to complete her last rites. It was rejected. How unlucky I was… a person who could not see his mother in her last days, and who could not even show up at her cremation.

My father came to meet me after a year and all he had for me was curses. When I asked him if Hardik had given him the money, he said no, and as a result, my mother did not receive treatment on time. That night I cried a lot. I asked my father to appeal in the High Court, but it was too late. A clause mentioned in the conviction papers said that I had one month's time from the date of sentencing to appeal to the High Court. That window had closed a long time ago.

That's when I came to know about Garima, who had changed her name to Varunika after achieving success. She had married Hardik.

Dad died three years later. Thankfully, the court allowed me to cremate him. My father still had my mother's ashes to immerse. Thus, on that same day, I had the sorrowful task of bidding them both goodbye amidst a veil of tears.

After that, each day in jail I used to think about Garima and Hardik, and my anger kept getting stronger and stronger. All I wanted was for them to be dead by my hands. Fourteen years in jail is enough time to plan the perfect murder and execute it. I was left-handed but started using my right hand to become ambidextrous. It was to play the most important role in my revenge plot. Tracing that liar and cheat, Varunika, and her low-life husband was not difficult. Also, I did not want another innocent person to end up behind bars, and that's why lied about Saransh's whereabouts. Actually, I was not in the cabin at that time."

Chapter – 23

Chandrika's Story

Kishan held back his tears and sat staring at the burning logs. I felt deeply sorry for him and kept quiet for quite some time.

"Now, what is your plan?" I broke the ice.

"You tell me, madam. I have already said what I had to say," Kishan said in a meek voice.

Kishan had figured out what was going on inside me. I could not make a decision.

"Madam, if you are confused, I suggest the first thing you must do is take off your make up and change your clothes."

I turned on my mobile, put the camera in selfie mode and gazed at my lovely face. I was so mesmerized by my new avatar that it was difficult for me to come to terms with my actual face. If it had all been a dream, I wanted to live it life-long, and did not want to wake up.

Kishan studied my face and understood my dilemma. He threw a few more logs onto the fire to warm up the place further.

"Madam, when you left your phone here by mistake, your speaker was on and I heard your father speaking on the other side."

I shrugged. Kishan continued, "He was talking about Daksha who studied with you in school and how you both used to feed small puppies. With great difficulty you had connected with him again, but now he is going out of country for one year or something like that."

I stood up. My legs felt like crumbling logs of wood. I looked at Kishan and said, "It doesn't matter if I have consumed liquor or not, I have lost my control in any case. If you try to escape, believe me you will meet my bullet and it will make a hole in your head. I don't care about my punishment."

After that, I went to the washroom and cleaned my face, scrubbing hard to bring it back to normal. Once again, I wore my pride-inducing police uniform.

༄ ༄ ༄

I went to the kitchen and asked Ishwar to make me some strong black coffee to clear my head. When I went back to the fire I saw that Kishan was still there. I called my father immediately and he replied curtly, "Hello!"

I was taken aback by his tone and did not reply for a few minutes. Papa kept quiet but waited on the line. He then asked me lovingly, "You are crying, aren't you?" I kept quiet. Papa asked again, "Chandrika, I am your Papa and I know your habits very well. I am sure you are crying." My father heard my silent cries.

When he spoke again his voice had more compassion, and he said, "When you were small, you would always come to me, what happened today? "

A long silence followed. Papa decided to break it. He wanted me to rid myself of my guilt and come out of my sorrow. So, he sang a song from a movie. This was his way of cheering me up whenever I was depressed. He started with one line and continued to the next...

"*Sooraj na ban paye toh...* (If you cannot become the sun)"

I kept mum and my father repeated, "*Sooraj na ban paye toh...?*"

Then, I mustered some courage, and replied in a trembling voice, "...*Banke deepak jalta chal...*(Make yourself into a small star to light the path.)"

Papa continued, "*Phool mile ya angare...*(Don't worry whether you get happiness or sorrow.)"

I replied again, in the same voice, "...*Sach ki rahon pe chalta chal.* (Keep following the path of truth.)"

"I am your bad girl, Papa," my voice cracked.

"No… no. You are not. Whatever your decision is, I am sure you have a very good reason for it. Am proud of you everything you have done and are doing. This is God's will. You are being given a divine exam. Do your work honestly and never think about winning or losing."

I got a lot of strength and confidence after talking to my father as he is the only inspiration in my life. If I had spoken to Papa earlier, this situation would have never come about.

"Daksha is the same person I loved, and just two days ago you told me to set up my engagement; furthermore, you did not provide me his phone number. As a result, I was left in the dark regarding Daksha. I had a five-minute phone conversation with him, scarcely speaking.

"That was a planned surprise for you. Even your mother was unaware of this. I knew you'd never say *No* to me. It is only Daksha's family and I who are aware of it. Once you told me about your crush, from that day, I started searching for your lost Prince."

"You are my great Papa."

"Yes, I am."

"Papa, if you have Daksha's number, please WhatsApp it."

"I will do that for sure, my strong child."

"One more thing, Papa. Be ready with your Chivas Regal."

"Are you quitting this job too?"

"Yes, Papa. In order to clear my IPS exam, I have to resign from this job."

Papa laughed loudly for me, undoubtedly in support of my decision. I too had a wide smile on my face.

꙰ ꙰ ꙰

Past | Day 1 | 11:00 PM

My eyes were still wet and when I finally called Daksha. My love came flooding back along with running tears.

"Hello."

"I apologize that I kept you and your family waiting for me," I said between sobs. I was regretting a lot of decisions that I had made. I could feel my love, my first, flow through the phone. It felt like my body was exuding a fragrance of happiness and joy. I wanted Daksha to embrace me tightly in his arms and engulf me in his love. There was silence for a minute and after that Daksha stammered, "It's okay... I understand."

"You are leaving for a year tomorrow to become a cyber-security expert and I could not even make it to meet you."

"No problem, Chandrika. I told you, it's okay," he responded.

I wiped my tears away with my palms, "But… but… I look so ugly."

"No problem… it's okay." Daksha responded in the same tone once more.

I got a little irritated and scolded him softly, "Do you know how to say anything else or only this one line?"

Daksha thought for a moment and replied, "I like you."

"Only… *like?*"

"Hmm… I have liked you ever since we were in school, but now I love you."

"Oh! I thought you only love your work."

"I do, but work comes second to you," Daksha laughed and I joined in too.

"What happened to those puppies after I left school?"

"You still remember? I nurtured them till my vacation started."

"Like our love…" Daksha interrupted, and I stopped for a moment.

"When I returned after that, there were no puppies to be seen. All those puppies were adopted by dog lovers."

I looked at Kishan and said, "Daksha, I will call you later. Right now, I have to go. I am busy with a case. Hope you understand."

"Go! Do what you have to do… and good luck."

Tears rolled down my cheeks. Only this time they melted into my happy smile. I hung up the phone.

❧ ❧ ❧

I wiped the pearls of joy from my face and went back to where Kishan was. "Do you have any plan to set right what you have messed up?"

Kishan had no answer. He just kept quiet and coughed for some time.

I was in a dilemma, though. Dogra sir had already given the name of the accused as Saransh, so the police would be working full time to prove him guilty. After all it was Dogra sir's and their image and credibility at stake. In that case, Saransh would not be released from custody. Also, if I provided Kishan's name as the culprit, it would be an injustice because he had already served a life sentence for a crime he did not commit.

I looked at my watch and called Daksha again to get his help. After five minutes, I asked Kishan, "Where is the phone from which you used to call Varunika?"

Kishan went to his room and returned with the phone. This was the phone he had used to send WhatsApp messages to Varunika.

First, I removed the SIM card from Kishan's phone and inserted my second SIM into it, pressed the button and opened WhatsApp. In order to copy the data, I ran an app on the phone. I powered off Kishan's phone, extracted my SIM, and inserted his SIM again.

It was now 12:00 AM on my watch. Kishan looked at me like he wanted to ask what I was doing.

"Charge this phone, it is low on battery," I said. Kishan nodded.

I came closer to him, "Listen carefully. I have installed a program on your phone. Tomorrow morning, if Saransh is proven guilty, I will give a missed call to my fiancé, and as soon as he activates his phone, a message will be triggered automatically. The police team will trace the phone to his number and will definitely send a team to that location."

"…and the police will be forced to shift their suspicions to someone other than Saransh, so he will not be a suspect anymore," Kishan concluded.

"Correct. By the way, do you know any safe place where we can keep your mobile?"

"Yes, there is an old hut nearby where no one stays."

❄ ❄ ❄

Around 2:00 AM, when the constables were drowsy and inattentive, I suggested to Kishan that he plant the phone. He took out his phone which was fully charged by then and was about to head off when he stopped, took some dry leaves, and rubbed them all over his body. Then he put some wet logs of wood into the fire that made the smoke and fumes rise up. Then stood front of that fire.

I asked, "Are you doing all this to confuse the sniffer dogs."

Kishan nodded. "I will repeat the same process once I come back. The dogs are trained to smell specific scents, like humans, clothes, and other items. When your body scent is masked by natural scents, they get confused and run around in circles."

❀❀❀

Present | Day 2 | 11:15 AM

Ishwar comes to see Chandrika off. Chandrika stops her bike near the security guard's cabin and Kishan pushes the barricade aside to clear the way for her.

"What will you do now?"

"I don't know, madam. I think I too will leave this place after a day or two, once I receive my money." Kishan coughs.

"You do not have TB so drop the act. I hope that you will apply your knowledge to positive things from now on. I am unable to change the past, but I hope that in future you will follow the path of honesty and truth," Chandrika advises Kishan and he nods.

"One more thing, on that stormy day, no truck passed in front of this road. A perfect murder doesn't exist. It is just an illusion in the mind of every murderer. Some clues will inevitably be left behind, and responsible investigators will always succeed in catching them. Remember one thing always. I will keep a watch on you. I have your address and will check on you."

Kishan nodded.

अर्क अर्क अर्क

Eight months later…

After the completion of her remand time, the police filed a charge sheet against Varunika. She was convicted for conspiracy to murder Hardik and was sent back to jail. The police could not find the murder weapon or the mysterious guy.

Chandrika is exiting the IPS examination center and decides to check on Kishan.

She travels to his hamlet, eager to see what he has been up to recently.

Chandrika approaches the door and knocks, but no one answers her.

"Are you blind?" The door is locked." A 12-year-old boy says while tapping a ball with a broken cricket bat.

"Oh!" Chandrika notices the lock and immediately asks, "Where is he?"

"Bhaiya (brother) passed away. We could not sleep at night; he was coughing too much," the boy says.

His mother comes out of the house next door when she sees her son talking to an unfamiliar person.

"What do you want, madam?"

Chandrika gestures to the lock.

"Kishan *bhaiya* passed away two months ago."

Chandrika is shocked.

"Who are you and why are you inquiring about him?" The woman adjusts her sari while her son goes back to playing with the ball.

Chandrika introduces herself.

"So you're in the police?"

When she confirms it, the neighbour goes into her house and comes out after a few minutes with a brown envelope that she hands over to Chandrika. Chandrika sees that it is addressed to her.

Controlling her emotions, Chandrika asks, "How did he die?"

"He was a TB patient."

"Did he not consult the doctor?"

"His treatment had already begun, but when he returned to this village, he stopped taking the medicines that he had been prescribed. You tell me, madam, how is it possible for a patient to be cured without medicine?"

Chandrika does not reply. She thanks the neighbour and leaves. After driving a little way, she stops her bike near a water channel and opens the envelope.

"Madam," Kishan's letter reads, "I know you will come to see me. Unfortunately, I will not be around by then. You will get only this letter. During my imprisonment, I witnessed only crooked and greedy policemen and concluded that there are no honest police officers in our system. However, once I met you, I began believing that honest police officers do exist.

You are right, no murder is flawless. Even perfect criminals leave some clues behind. After coming home, I was certain of one thing: if, one day, an honest police officer is assigned to solve this case, they will certainly find me, and Varunika will be released. My revenge took a higher precedence than my life. My life was sacrificed for retribution. I've decided to die and leave no hints. I want Varunika to pay for her crimes. I have stopped my medicines and now I am in the last stage of my life.

Goodbye,

Aadarsh."

Chandrika reads the letter a couple of times, then tears it into small pieces. She throws the bits into the water channel. Then, she feels something inside the envelope. When she blows into the envelope, she finds a green color sharpener. She glances at it and throws the sharpener into the field. A lone tear rolls down Chandrika's cheeks and she mumbles, ***now it is the perfect murder.***

❈ ❈ ❈